Acquisition & Surrender

A BDSM Workplace Erotic Romance Novel

April Cross

TWISTED ROSE
PUBLISHING

Contents

CHAPTER 1

The email hits my inbox at 8:37 on Monday morning.

IMPORTANT: All-Hands Meeting—9:00 AM. Attendance Mandatory.

The pen in my fingers freezes mid-twirl. Mandatory. In corporate speak, that translates to *start updating your resumes.*

Keyboards stutter, then go silent. Conversations die as the news spreads, and people swivel in their chairs toward their screens. Sandra from HR power-walks past my cubicle without acknowledging my existence.

Not that I expected anything different since I've perfected the art of being invisible here. Invisible keeps me safe. Forgettable keeps me employed. No one notices when I eat lunch alone at my desk or stay two hours late because there's nowhere else to be.

My birthday was last month. Sandra sent the standard company-wide email with the generic cake emoji. Exactly zero people stopped by my desk. I bought myself a cupcake from the lobby café and ate it in the copier room so no one would see I was celebrating alone.

Twenty-six years of learning that forgettable is better than being remembered and then discarded anyway.

But it's time to get this meeting over with so I can polish up that resume. As I follow everyone heading toward the conference room, I rehearse the words I'll need when they hand me a cardboard box.

Thanks for having me. Take care.

Christ. Even my imaginary send-off is pathetic.

The hallway is a blur of anxious faces and whispered speculation. Marcus from accounting catches my eye, and for half a second, I think he might say a word. Maybe acknowledge that we've worked on the same floor for three years and it's all about to end.

He looks away.

Right. Invisible. Funny how it stings when it actually works.

The conference room is packed. I wedge myself into the corner near the door out of habit. Always know your exit. Always have a plan for when they decide you're not needed anymore.

I catch my reflection in the glass partition. Hair scraped into its usual low bun because I woke up late. Brown eyes that look perpetually tired because they are. I tug at my collar and smooth my skirt. Like being presentable matters when the axe is about to fall.

Richard, our CEO, stands at the front of the room looking like he aged a decade overnight. He won't meet anyone's eyes, and his hands tremble when he adjusts his glasses. I recognize that tremor. It comes from knowing you're about to disappoint people.

Been there. Am there. Will probably always be there.

"Good morning, everyone. As of this morning, Mercer and Associates has entered into an acquisition agreement with Ashford Holdings."

The room erupts, and a guy spills his coffee somewhere to my left. A woman near me whispers, "Oh God," like she's praying.

Ashford Holdings. Even I know that name. They acquire struggling companies and gut them. Restructure. Polite words for *you're fired, enjoy your pathetic severance.*

Lydia Kessler, Senior Director for Mercer and Associates, stands near the front. She's always immaculate, the kind of woman who makes the rest of us feel like we're playing dress-up. Her small smile says she's not upset about what's happening.

My hands go cold, and I shove them under my thighs. Three years of keeping my head down and doing good work that no one noticed. Three years of convincing myself that stability was worth more than recognition, that being overlooked was a survival strategy, not a slow death.

And now none of it matters anyway.

Richard drones on. Phrases like *exciting opportunity* and *moving forward together* drift past without landing. Corporate lullabies for a funeral.

The conference door opens, and the low murmur of voices cuts off like a switch has been thrown.

The man who walks in is terrifying. Logically, I know this. He's the reason Richard looks like he hasn't slept in days. But my body perks up like a puppy seeing its owner. Apparently, my libido has a death wish.

He's over six feet with shoulders broad enough to block out the fluorescent glare. Dark hair with silver threading at the temples. Gray eyes, cold and assessing. He moves with the kind of command that makes my nipples tighten against my bra, and when he scans the room, every nerve in my body sparks alive. I press my thighs together and hate myself a little.

His attention sweeps the crowded space. Cataloging. Deciding who's worth keeping and who's dead weight.

Without thinking, I tilt my chin down. My body softens the same way it did when my old manager used to yell, except this is different. This is a voluntary reflex I didn't know I had.

I jerk my head up and force my shoulders square. What the hell was that?

I don't fight against authority—I've never had the spine for that. I learned young that fighting back just makes foster parents send you somewhere worse. So I comply just enough to stay invisible while keeping the real me locked somewhere they can't touch. Every supervisor and every boyfriend who thought he knew better—same strategy of surface compliance and nothing real.

But that wasn't strategic. That was surrender. And some part of me *wanted* it. Which is information I don't know what to do with. My pulse kicks hard against my ribs. My response should feel wrong, but it doesn't. That's the problem.

When his gaze finally reaches my corner, it stops. On me. He can't actually be looking at *me.* I'm the person people accidentally forget to CC on company emails. The one who gets left off lunch orders. The one whose name takes two tries to remember.

Heat floods my cheeks and arrows down, settling hot between my thighs.

I look away first. I'm not up to playing chicken with a billionaire. I'd lose. My therapist would have thoughts about this. If I could afford one.

When I risk another glance, he's striding toward Richard with his hand extended. Blood rushes hot through my veins. The flush won't fade.

Then I notice his hands. God, his hands. Long, thick fingers. I can already imagine them fisted in my hair, forcing my chin up. My clit pulses, a slow, insistent beat I can't ignore. He hasn't said a word, and I'm getting wet for the executioner.

"Thank you, Richard." The man's voice is smooth and carries without effort. "I'll take it from here."

Richard practically trips over himself retreating. Twelve years of building this company, and he steps aside like a man who's already cashed his buyout check.

Three people join the man up front. A woman with a lanyard that reads TESSA HOLBROOK scans the room. Her expression is warmer, like she's checking if everyone's okay rather than cataloging assets. The man beside her has an easy slouch. He catches my eye for a split second, and there's kindness there before he looks away.

Weird. People don't usually notice me enough to be kind.

A younger woman flanks his other side. Her dark hair is pulled into a messy bun that says she has better things to do than worry about appearances. She's scrolling through her phone like she's ready for the meeting to be over with. When she glances up, she smiles at the guy with the kindness in his eyes, and I can tell they're good friends.

"I'm Sebastian Ashford." The commanding guy speaks as if anyone in this room doesn't know. "I'm not here to dismantle what you've built. I'm here because I see potential."

His gaze finds me again and holds a second too long while I forget how to breathe. Yep, I'm soaked and aching for the man signing the pink slips. This is a new low, even for me. I'm going to need new panties after this meeting, and I can't expense that. Can you expense dignity? Asking for a friend who is definitely not the woman sitting in the corner having inappropriate thoughts about the new boss's hands.

"The question is whether you're willing to rise to meet it."

His voice has authority that doesn't ask for respect. It commands it.

He's still talking. Mission statements and growth trajectories and words that should matter more than the way his shoulders fill out that jacket. Someone near me is crying quietly while I'm aroused to the point of distraction. We're all processing this differently, I guess.

Yet another traitorous part of me wants to earn his respect. I want to prove I'm worth whatever attention he's giving me, even though wanting to be seen by him is the worst idea I've had in a long time. And I once convinced myself that dating my college TA would end well.

The meeting dissolves into agitated clusters. Colleagues I've barely spoken to suddenly want to bond over shared dread. I nod at a few sympathetic glances, murmur a response that means nothing.

I'm already calculating how fast I can get to my desk to job hunt. Early bird gets the best job, or however the expression goes. I slip out the door, but the hallway is clogged with people trying to escape. I weave around a cluster near the elevator and nearly collide with expensive charcoal fabric.

"Careful."

One word. Close. Way too close.

A firm hand grips my elbow before I can stumble. Warm and large enough to wrap completely around my arm. The contact sends a bolt of heat down my spine.

Sebastian Ashford looks down at me, and every coherent thought in my head evaporates.

Fuck.

This close, I can see the way his jaw tightens as he studies me. His cologne hits me. Cedar and smoke. He smells like a warning I'm not going to heed. He still hasn't let go.

I need to apologize and retreat. Be the forgettable employee I've trained myself to be.

"I—sorry." It comes out embarrassingly breathy. "I wasn't watching where I was going."

"No." His thumb brushes the inside of my elbow. "You weren't."

Heat floods my face, and my knees wobble. My body has apparently decided to betray me in every possible way today.

Every survival instinct I've honed over twenty-six years says *step away from the man who now controls your paycheck*. But my feet have forgotten how to work.

Worse, I don't want them to remember.

The urge to stay here, to wait until he dismisses me, rises so powerfully within me I nearly choke on it. I want to apologize again. Lower my eyes. Ask if there's anything I can do to make this right. Instincts that don't belong to me are suddenly running the show.

When did I start needing permission to leave? And more importantly, wanting permission from this stranger?

The thought is so foreign, so wrong, that when he releases my elbow, I force my feet to shuffle backward. One step. Then another. Distance. I need distance.

"You were in the meeting. In the corner. Near the door."

"I was trying to be inconspicuous." The words slip out before I can stop them.

One eyebrow rises. "Then you failed."

His gaze drops to my throat and lingers. Can he see my pulse hammering?

My body goes very still. The urge to tilt my chin and show him more of my throat claws at me. This is insane. Absolutely unhinged. I have clearly lost my mind since that email hit my inbox.

"Your name."

It's not a question. It's a command. And god help me, I answer immediately.

"Elise. Elise Hart."

His lips curve. Not quite a smile. More like he's filing the information away.

"Elise." His voice drops, and my name in his mouth sounds like a claim. "I'll remember that."

Then he walks away without another word.

I stand in the hallway, flushed and trembling and already wanting more. What the hell have I gotten myself into?

When I get back to my desk, my email inbox flashes with a notification.

E. Hart - Please report to Mr. Ashford's office at 8:00 AM tomorrow.

I read it three times.

Tomorrow at eight o'clock, I'll be meeting with the man who makes me forget how to breathe.

I tell myself I need to update my resume and plan my escape route. But in the back of my mind, I can't stop myself from counting the minutes and hating myself for how much I want them to pass faster.

CHAPTER 2

Sleep won't come. My mind keeps circling back to Sebastian Ashford and tomorrow's meeting. I stare at the ceiling, replaying every second in the hallway. His hand on my elbow. The way he said my name. The way my body still responds to the memory, wet and aching hours later.

By 1 a.m., I give up and slide my hand between my legs while imagining he's commanding me to kneel and suck his cock. His hands are in my hair, and he's telling me exactly what to do before he pulls me up and bends me over his desk.

I come twice. Both times imagining him fucking me over various pieces of office furniture.

I fall asleep, only to wake at 4 a.m. and do it again because apparently, I'm shameless and have a thing for authority figures.

When my alarm finally drags me up for good, I'm standing in front of my closet at 5:47 a.m. with a desperate ache between my legs that three orgasms couldn't satisfy. Every dress I own suddenly seems wrong. Too conservative. Too revealing. Too *I was up all night finger fucking myself over my new boss.*

I settle on a navy skirt and white blouse. Professional. Fitted enough to suggest a body but not enough to scream desperation.

The woman in the mirror has flushed cheeks and bright eyes. She looks like someone about to do something catastrophically stupid if given the chance.

That's accurate.

By 7:30, I'm in line at the coffee stand buying two coffees. I need caffeine so I can sound like a competent adult when I see him. Not like someone who spent last night coming three times to the memory of his hand on my arm.

The executive floor is the same as always with its plush carpet and soft lighting. Someone I don't recognize passes me. I'm suddenly convinced they can tell my blouse cost twelve dollars and I don't belong here. I don't know why I care since I'm about to get fired.

His door is open.

I stop at the threshold, balancing both coffee cups, and my lungs forget how to function.

Sebastian's at his desk, jacket discarded, sleeves rolled to his elbows. Morning light catches the silver at his temples and the corded muscles of his forearms. He's reading, pen in hand, and hasn't noticed me yet.

His hands. Those long, thick fingers wrapped around that pen. The same hands I imagined on me last night. In me. Controlling me.

My nipples tighten, and heat pools low in my belly. I'm already wet, and he hasn't even looked at me.

Get it together. This is a meeting about your job. About your future. About anything other than how badly you want to know what his hands would feel like pinning you down.

He looks up. His gray eyes lock on mine, and every rational thought evaporates. I shift my weight to hide the fact I'm pressing my thighs together.

"You're early." His voice is steady. Mine won't be.

"Should I—" I nod vaguely toward the hallway. "Come back?"

"No." He sets down the pen. "Close the door. Sit."

Two commands. My mouth speaks before my brain catches up.

"Yes, Sir." The word escapes before I can catch it. My face flames. I've said "sir" plenty of times in my life and it never felt like *that*. We're in his office. He's my boss. And I—

"What did you call me?"

"I—nothing. I didn't mean—" The words tangle in my throat. I want a portal to open up and take me to another dimension or at least rewind the last two minutes.

"Say it again."

The command is soft. The authority behind it isn't.

Butterflies zoom in my stomach, and I whisper, "Sir."

Satisfaction flickers across his face before he drops his gaze back to the folder and acts like nothing happened.

But I caught it. The dilation of his pupils. The way his jaw tightened with barely-restrained control.

Now all I can think about is what other words would earn me that look.

I finally close the door and cross to the chair in front of his desk, setting both coffees on the surface before I sit.

"I didn't know how you took it. One's black, one has cream."

He glances at the cups. "Which do you prefer?"

"Oh, it doesn't matter." I shrug. "Whichever you don't want is fine."

His gaze lifts to mine and holds. "That's not what I asked."

My skin prickles and the room is suddenly too warm. "I meant you should take whichever one you like. I'm happy with either."

"You're happy with whatever's left over." He reaches for the black coffee and takes a slow sip, watching me over the rim. "That usually means *I won't risk having a preference.*"

I fight the urge to fidget because he's right. And his being right is making me wetter.

"Drink your coffee, Elise." It's not said unkindly. "It's too early in the morning to be uncomfortable over caffeine."

I wrap both hands around the cup because I need to hold onto anything that isn't him. The warmth grounds me. Barely.

"You didn't sleep well last night," he says.

My breath catches, pulse spiking. "What makes you—?"

"You look tired, but your cheeks are flushed and your eyes are bright. You've pressed your thighs together twice since you walked in here." He leans back in his chair, fingers steepled. "That's not anxiety."

Oh god. He's been watching me squirm. He knows exactly what state I'm in, and probably why.

"I—" The word dies in my throat.

"You weren't up all night worrying about this meeting, were you?"

He already knows the answer, and my intuition says he's waiting to see if I'll lie.

I can't. Not with those gray eyes pinning me in place.

"No," I whisper.

"Good." Approval flashes across his face, and he slides a folder across the desk. "Then let's talk about your future."

My hands tremble as I open it.

"You still have a job. A better one."

The paperwork inside says Senior Analyst. Direct report to the CEO. Access to proprietary data across all acquisitions. Monthly presentations to the executive team.

The salary is thirty percent more than I make now.

"This is—" I shake my head. "Why me?"

"Because you're capable of more than anyone here realizes. Including you." He leans forward, elbows on the desk. "I read your file and looked at your quarterly reports last night. Impressive work. You've been flying under the radar. That ends now."

The words sink in. He sees me—really sees me—and he won't let me hide.

"What if I'm not ready?"

"You're ready." He holds my gaze. "Are you going to trust me or listen to the voice in your head that's convinced you you're not enough? Your choice."

My throat tightens. He's not coddling me. "I want to trust you. I'll try."

"Good girl."

Two words. They hit me like a match to gasoline.

Every nerve ending ignites at once. Desire tightens in my core and spirals outward. My skin burns. My clit pulses. Heat crawls up my throat as my lips part, and I can't hide any of it. No one has ever made me react like this with just words.

His gaze sharpens. For three heartbeats, neither of us moves.

"Elise." His voice is rougher now. "What happened when I called you that?"

Oh god, do I have to say it?

"I'm not asking to embarrass you. But if you're going to work under me, I need to know. Discomfort or interest?"

Under him...yeah, it's messed up how much I want him. The smart move would be to say it's fine, that I'm completely uninterested.

Except, I've spent my whole life pretending. I'm suddenly tired of wondering what would happen if I were honest.

"Interest." My voice is barely a whisper.

"Say it clearly."

"I liked it." I force myself to hold his gaze. "I liked it a lot."

His jaw tightens, control rippling visibly beneath his skin. For a moment, neither of us speaks.

"Lock the door."

My heart stutters. I rise on trembling legs and lock the door. The click reverberates through me. Back at my chair, I stay on my feet.

"I need to tell you something." He comes around the desk, stopping in front of me. "I'm a Dominant. Do you know what that means?"

"I've read things." And felt things around him I didn't even know were inside me.

"Reading isn't the same as experiencing."

He's standing close enough that I have to tilt my head to hold his gaze. Close enough that I can smell him, the cedar and smoke that makes every rational thought fly out the window.

I don't let myself think. If I think, I'll talk myself out of it.

I sink to my knees.

The carpet is soft beneath me, and I'm eye-level with his belt. There's an obvious bulge straining against his slacks.

My mouth waters. I did that. "Then show me."

Sebastian goes completely still. I look up at him, terrified and exhilarated and probably crazy. And maybe about to lose my job. But this feels right.

His chest rises and falls. His jaw works like he's swallowing words.

"Elise." His voice is strained. "You don't know what you're asking for."

"Maybe not, but I've spent my whole life being reasonable." The words tumble out, desperate. "Playing it safe. Following the rules. And it's gotten me exactly nowhere." I press my palms against my thighs to keep from reaching for him. "I don't want safe anymore."

He's silent for a long moment. Then his hand slides into my hair and his fingers curl against my scalp.

"If you want this—if you want me—you need to understand what you're agreeing to. When we're alone, I'll expect your submission. Your trust. When I ask, you let me take control."

His thumb presses against my temple. He can feel me trembling.

"What does that look like?" My voice shakes.

"It looks like you doing what I tell you. Kneeling when I ask." His grip tightens slightly. "It looks like me learning exactly how your body responds and using that knowledge to take you apart."

My clit throbs. I'm so wet I can tell my panties are shot...again.

"Yes." The word comes out breathless. "I want that. I want you."

"We need to establish boundaries first." He brushes his thumb over my bottom lip, and I risk sneaking my tongue out to taste his skin—salt and warmth—before retreating.

He groans. "If at any point you want to stop, you say red. I don't care if we're in the middle of something. You say the color red, and everything stops. Understood?"

"Yes, Sir."

The word slips out again, and his eyes glitter.

When he drops his hand from my face, for one terrible second, I think I've blown it. Oh fuck, he's going to tell me to collect my stuff from my desk.

Then he speaks. "Stand up."

I obey.

"I'm going to kiss you before we continue this discussion."

His hand finds the nape of my neck. Fingers thread into my hair. He tilts my head to the exact angle he wants, and then his mouth claims mine.

It's not tentative. He kisses me like he's been thinking about it for hours, like he's already mapped out every response my body will give him. His tongue slides against mine, coaxing and commanding at once, and I make a needy, desperate sound I've never heard from my own throat.

The world dissolves. There's only the heat of his mouth, the firmness of his grip, the way he commands every sensation. I can't think. Can't breathe. Can't do anything but surrender to the feeling consuming me.

When he finally pulls away, I chase his mouth before I can stop myself. My knees buckle. He catches me, hands gripping my waist.

"That went straight to my—" I stop and swallow. "Everywhere."

"Everywhere." His voice drops. "Say it properly."

"My pussy." The word comes out shaky.

"Do you have any idea what you do to me?"

I shake my head.

"I've been thinking about you since yesterday. Thinking about what it would be like to hear you beg." His grip tightens on my waist. "I've imagined what you'd look like on your knees for me."

My whole body throbs. I want to drop to my knees right now. I want his hand in my hair and his cock in my mouth while he calls me a good girl.

He kisses me again, harder this time. His hand fists in my hair. The sharp sting makes me gasp, and he swallows the sound while taking everything I have to give.

When he breaks the kiss off, I'm trembling.

"Sebastian. Please."

"Please what?"

I don't know. I ache so badly I can't think straight.

He releases my waist and takes a half step away. "What do you want, Elise?"

I want him to know what I need before I do. I want him to tell me what to do without me having to ask for it.

And then I realize—suddenly, with absolute clarity—that I know exactly what I really want.

I've been wanting it since he walked into that conference room. Since his gaze found mine in the corner. Since his hand closed around my elbow in the hallway.

I sink to my knees again in front of him, but this time, I know why.

"Elise." His voice is stunned. "I didn't ask you to—"

"I know." I look up at him, pulse racing. "I want this."

His eyes blaze with lust while his jaw ticks.

"You said you imagined me on my knees for you." My voice is steadier than I expected.

For a long moment, he stares down at me. "Beautiful." The word is quiet. Almost reverent. "You have no idea how perfect you look like this."

Warmth floods through me. Nobody has ever called me beautiful while I'm on my knees. Nobody has ever looked at me like I'm precious.

"I want to taste you. Please let me."

His control cracks. I can see it fracturing behind his eyes.

"We're going to go slow." His voice is rough. Strained. "If anything is too much, you tap my thigh twice." He waits. "Show me."

I tap his thigh twice.

"Perfect."

His praise makes my head spin, and I spread my knees slightly, hoping to ease the ache.

He undoes his belt. The buckle releases with a sharp metallic click that cuts through the silence. When he opens his pants and pulls his cock free, it's thick, flushed dark, and the head is already wet. Mmm, yummy. Seeing him like this—hard because of me, in his office where anyone could knock—makes my pulse spike with equal parts recklessness and desire.

I lean forward, not waiting for permission. When my lips touch the head of his cock, he tastes like salt and skin. I part my lips wider and the sound that escapes me is pure need. I didn't expect to want him this badly.

"Fuck." The word punches out of him. "Your mouth."

I take him deeper and hollow my cheeks. The stretch makes my jaw ache, and it's good. I feel powerful. I'm exactly where I want to be. Doing exactly what I want to do.

This is me choosing.

"That's it." He slides his fingers into my hair. "Take what you can."

I take him deeper. His hips roll forward, finding a rhythm. Each slow thrust fills the office with wet, filthy sounds.

I'm drenched and my thighs are slick. My clit throbs with every pulse of my heartbeat. I've never been this desperate, this empty and needing to be filled. But this isn't about me right now. This is about making him lose control.

My tongue swirls around the head each time I pull away. One hand wraps around what I can't take, the other clenches his thigh. His firm grip in my hair guides me.

I've given blowjobs before. Perfunctory things. Obligations.

This is nothing like that.

This is power. His pleasure in my hand and mouth. Every groan I drag from him is a victory that I feel between my own legs.

"So fucking good." His moan vibrates through me. "Just like that."

I take him as deep as I can, relaxing my throat, and his control shatters. His breathing goes ragged. His thrusts become quicker and shorter as his cock swells against my tongue.

"I'm close," he growls. "Elise, where do you want—?"

I answer by taking him deeper. By meeting his eyes and refusing to look away.

I don't want him to hold back.

He comes hard with a guttural groan. Hot spurts of cum coat my tongue, and I swallow it down, throat working. I don't stop. My hand clasps his thighs as the muscles tremor. His breathing slows, and he loses his grip in my hair as he pulls his cock from my mouth.

For a long moment, neither of us moves. Then he reaches down and cups my face with both hands, tilting my head up.

His expression is unguarded. "Why?" His thumbs brush my cheekbones.

"I wanted to." My voice is hoarse.

He pulls me to my feet, and my legs wobble. He steadies me with an arm around my waist and leads me to the leather couch in the corner of his office.

"Sit."

I obey. He grabs a bottle of water from a side table next to the couch, settles beside me, and pulls me against his chest. His heartbeat is steady beneath my ear.

He opens the bottle. "Drink."

It's a command, but there's care behind it. He guides it to my lips, and I take a sip before taking the bottle from him.

When I finish half the bottle, he gently untangles my hair where his grip twisted it. His fingers work through the strands with tenderness that makes my chest ache.

Then he takes my hands in his and turns them over.

"What are you—?"

"Checking." His thumb traces over where my nails dug crescents into my own palms. "You were clenching your fist hard."

I look down at the faint pink marks in my palm. I didn't even notice.

"Did I hurt you?" There's genuine concern in his voice.

"No." I shake my head. "I didn't realize I was doing it."

He lifts my hand to his mouth. Presses his lips to the center of my palm, right over the marks.

The gesture is so tender it steals my breath. This—this checking, this gentleness after—feels almost more intimate than having his cock in my mouth.

"How are you?" His lips brush my temple. "Honestly."

I take stock. My lips are puffy. I'm wet and throbbing, still desperate for release.

But underneath all of that is peace. For the first time in my life, I took what I wanted.

"I'm not second-guessing myself."

His arm tightens around me. "Good."

We sit in silence, and he strokes my hair while my breathing steadies.

"What happens now?" I ask quietly.

"Now you accept the job offer." His voice is pleased, almost amused. "The real conversations happen later. When we both have time to think clearly."

"And if I want more?"

He tilts my chin up and makes me meet his eyes.

"Then you tell me. Clearly. With words. And we negotiate what that looks like." His thumb traces my lower lip. "But right now, you need to process. So do I."

"Okay." I lean into his chest. "But for the record? I want more."

He laughs warmly. "Noted."

I close my eyes and let myself be held. For the first time in years, I don't feel invisible.

I feel chosen...and safe.

We sit like that for a few more minutes, but eventually he shifts. "I should get you out of here before people start wondering."

Right. Reality. The office.

He stands and offers me his hand. His fingers are gentle as he straightens my twisted hem.

Kneeling for him felt natural. This softness leaves me unsettled. I didn't expect gentleness.

"You did so well." His voice is quiet. "Thank you for trusting me."

"You're welcome," I whisper.

He opens the door, and I step into the hallway. I force myself to not look back, and when I get in the elevator, I sag against the wall.

Minutes ago, I was on my knees. Now I feel ten feet tall. My legs are shaking, but not from weakness. The tremor is electric. Alive. I made Sebastian Cole lose control. The knowledge fills a hollow space I didn't know I had.

My phone buzzes with a message.

Unknown: This is Sebastian. Text me when you get home tonight. I want to know you're okay.

My chest tightens as I add his number to my contacts.

He cares. Not about what I can give him, but about me.

A second text appears.

Sebastian: And Elise? Don't touch yourself. Next time you come, I'll be the one doing it.

I stare at my phone. My pussy throbs in protest, or maybe in agreement. My body has no loyalty.

This man is going to destroy me. In the best possible way. Or the worst. Jury's still out.

The kicker? I already know I'm going to let him.

It's going to be a long day of work.

Chapter 3

I've checked my phone forty-seven times since texting him last night to say I got home. That exact number because I started counting at check five when I realized I'd developed a Pavlovian response to notification sounds. Very normal behavior. Definitely not unhinged at all.

All he replied with was, "Good girl."

Now my pussy twitches every time my phone buzzes. This is not sustainable.

The spreadsheet on my screen hasn't changed in two hours. The same numbers stare at me. My coffee went cold at 9. It's 11:30 now, and my brain has decided those numbers are less interesting than remembering exactly what Sebastian's cum tasted like. Next time, I want it deep inside my pussy. I've officially lost my mind, but the view from insanity is surprisingly pleasant.

Two people walk past my cubicle and neither stops. For once, I'm grateful to be invisible. The dirty secret is probably written all over my face. *I blew our new boss yesterday and loved every second of it.*

My thighs press together. My body hasn't gotten the memo that we're at work. That we should be thinking about quarterly projections, not the way Sebastian's hand gripped my hair.

Good girl.

His voice echoes in my head, and I'm clenching around nothing, wet and aching in the middle of a Wednesday morning. My clit pulses like it has opinions about spreadsheets. It clearly thinks they're boring compared to Sebastian Ashford.

This is insane. I'm losing my mind over a man I've known for 48 hours.

My phone is face-up on my desk. Silent.

The HR email arrived earlier. The formal offer for Senior Analyst. Start date: Immediately.

I read it three times, signed the offer and returned it.

The promotion should be huge. Life-changing. It *is* life-changing. Everything I've secretly wanted: validation, security, proof I'm not replaceable.

But all I can think about is Sebastian and that damn text he sent. *Don't touch yourself. Next time you come, I'll be the one doing it.*

I didn't touch myself, but I wanted to. God, I wanted to. I laid in bed for an hour, throbbing, thinking about his cock in my mouth, and I still didn't do it because he told me not to.

The obedience surprises me. The way my body responds to his commands even when he's not there. I've had boyfriends, temporary men who passed through my life quickly, but I never wanted any of them to control me. I have no idea why I'm responding this way to Sebastian, and it doesn't scare me the way it probably should.

It makes me a horny, anxious mess with cold coffee and a job I can't focus on.

Very professional. My non-existent therapist would be so proud. I should probably get one with my raise. Do they make therapists specifically for *I sucked my boss's dick yesterday and now I can't focus on spreadsheets*? Asking for a me.

At 1:47, my phone buzzes.

Sebastian: Come to my office. We should talk.

That's it? No good afternoon, no warmth, no context. *We should talk.*

This is where he tells me it was a mistake. That I misread everything. That yesterday was a lapse in judgment, and I failed some test I didn't know I was taking—or maybe I sucked at sucking...

My phone buzzes again.

Sebastian: And stop catastrophizing. I can practically hear you spiraling from here.

The audacity of this man. If he can hear me spiraling from four floors up, he's either psychic or I'm that predictable. Both options are concerning.

I laugh at how stupid this is, and it's loud enough that the guy in the next cubicle looks over.

Pressing my lips together, I clear my throat and suppress another giggle as I respond.

Elise: I'm on my way.

Sebastian: Good.

He could have at least said "good girl." More proof he's about to end this.

I smooth my dress in the elevator and try to tame the butterflies in my chest. When he lets me down gently, I have to make sure I don't thank him for allowing me to give him a blow job.

His door is open again. Sebastian's behind his desk, jacket on. Professional. But his eyes find mine the second I appear, and heat ripples through me.

"Close the door. Sit."

My body obeys his commands on autopilot now. That's starting to seem less strange than it probably should.

"You've been catastrophizing since yesterday."

"I'm fine."

His eyebrow lifts. "Try again."

The gentle command cracks loose the panic. "I don't know what this is. I don't know what you want. I don't know if yesterday was—if I misread—"

"You didn't misread anything."

The certainty in his voice stops me cold.

"We moved fast," he continues. "Too fast for you to really know what you were agreeing to. We need to talk properly, but not here. Come to my place tonight. Seven o'clock. We'll negotiate."

"You want to end this." The words come out flat.

"No. I want to do this *right*." His voice drops, goes rougher. "Did you touch yourself last night?"

Warmth floods my face. "No."

"Good girl."

The praise goes straight to my pussy, arousal flooding me as my breathing catches audibly. I'm ready to roll over and beg. Pavlov would be so proud.

"Tonight," he says. "We establish rules. Nothing happens you don't agree to. Now go to work and try not to think about how badly I want to taste you."

Oh, fuck. I stand on shaky legs and at the door, I nearly collide with Tessa coming in.

She smiles warmly. "Welcome to the team, Elise."

Mumbling thanks, I flee to the elevator before my face gives everything away.

His building is glass and steel, with security that requires ID to enter the lobby. The doorman reads my name on my driver's license and escorts me to a private elevator, swiping his own card to send me up. The elevator only goes to one floor.

His floor.

I smooth my skirt for the third time. The same navy one I changed into after work. My armor.

The elevator opens directly into his condo, and I freeze.

Floor-to-ceiling windows overlook the city. A massive sectional in charcoal gray. Bookshelves lined with actual books, not decorator props. Colorful art on the walls that looks chosen because someone liked it, not because it was expensive.

This is where he lives. Where he sleeps. Where he probably walks around shirtless, drinking coffee in the morning. Mmm, shirtless...

Focus, Elise. You're here to talk, not fantasize about his abs. And it doesn't matter that you're hoping to see them.

Sebastian's standing by the windows, still in his work clothes minus the jacket. He turns when the elevator closes behind me.

"Elise." He crosses to me in three strides. "You're shaking."

Oh shit, I am. "I'm fine."

His hand curves around my elbow—the same spot he touched that first day—and warmth spreads up my arm. "When did you last eat?"

"I—what?"

"Food. When?"

"Lunch, I think. I don't—" Actually, did I eat lunch? I remember buying a sandwich. I don't remember eating it.

"Sit." He guides me toward the sectional with a hand on my lower back, every finger distinct through the fabric of my blouse.

He disappears into what must be the kitchen, and I'm left alone on his ridiculously comfortable couch. Twenty-six years old, and I still can't take care of myself. At least the foster system prepared me for this level of dysfunction. Gold star for consistency.

He returns with water and a plate—cheese, crackers, and strawberries—and sets them in front of me.

"Drink first. Then eat. We're not talking until you've done both."

It's not harsh. It's care. The command in his voice wraps around my chest and squeezes.

As I drink and eat, the shaking eases. He watches me the whole time, patient, and I don't realize how lightheaded I was until the food settles.

"Better?"

"Yes."

"Good girl."

The praise hits my clit like a tuning fork, and I flush, staring at the empty plate. If he keeps this up, I'm going to need new panties every time he approves of literally anything I do.

He takes the plate from me and sets it on the coffee table before taking my hand and lacing our fingers together. "Look at me."

I force my eyes up.

"I want you close for this conversation." He pats his thigh. "Come here."

My pulse trips. "You want me...in your lap?"

"Yes. We're going to talk about intimate things. I want to hold you while we do. Is that okay?"

In his lap. Where I can't escape. Where he'll notice every reaction. Where I'll be *held*.

"Yes."

I stand, and he guides me with hands on my waist, turning me so I'm sitting sideways across his thighs. One arm wraps around me. His other hand rests on my knee, thumb stroking small circles.

I kick my heels off and flex my toes. Thank god I painted my nails a soft pink last weekend.

Pretty," he murmurs, and I realize he's looking at my feet. Heat floods through me. His body is solid beneath me, and there's the very obvious evidence that this position affects him—a growing hardness against my ass that makes my body tingle.

"We're establishing the foundation we skipped," he says. "I'm going to ask questions. Some might be uncomfortable. You can say no to anything."

"Okay."

"First—what draws you to this? What actually pulls you toward submission?"

The question catches me off guard. I've been asking myself the same thing since yesterday.

"The quiet in my head," I say slowly. "When you tell me what to do, everything else...stops. All the noise and second-guessing. Is that weird?"

"No." His voice is warm. "The mental quiet you're describing—that's what we call subspace. Or the beginning of it. The rest of the world falls away, and there's only you and me and what I'm asking of you."

My chest tightens from happiness. He *gets* it.

He continues. "What do you want from this? Not what you think I want to hear. What do you actually want?"

"I want..." I stop for a moment and have to clear my throat. "I want safety. I want—"

"Keep going." His hand moves to my face, tipping my chin up.

"I want to belong to someone. To be chosen. To not be..." A hard swallow. "Forgettable."

His eyes soften. His thumb brushes my cheek, and I don't realize I'm crying until he wipes the tear away.

"You're the opposite of forgettable." His voice drops. "I've thought about you every hour since we met. Your little moans when we kissed. The way you trusted me. That's not forgettable. That's branded into my memory."

My thighs clench, and I know he notices.

"Now we talk about limits." His hand settles on my hip, grounding. "What do you know you don't want? Things that are off the table completely."

How do I know what I don't want? I quickly think of movies and books I've read, and the words come out in a rush, things I've thought about without realizing. "Um...no humiliation. Nothing where other people are watching us. Nothing that leaves permanent marks. No blood. I don't—" I take a breath. "I don't want to be shared."

His grip tightens on my hip. "I don't share." The words are possessive. "Ever. What's mine is mine. That's non-negotiable for me too."

Heat floods through me at the raw ownership of the word *mine*.

"What about things you're curious about but nervous?" he asks. "Soft limits. Things we could try with trust and communication."

I bite my lip. "Impact play. I've read about that. Spanking. Flogger."

"That's a perfect soft limit. We'll go slow and you'll tell me what works." His thumb traces circles on my hip. "Anything else?"

"Being tied up and blindfolds." The words comes out breathier than I intended. "I want to try those."

"Noted. Anything else?"

Oh god, this is a difficult conversation.

"I want to be told what to do. To earn praise. To..." I can barely get the words out. "To be owned."

There's a low growl in his throat, and for three heartbeats, neither of us moves.

"You're going to be the death of me," he says quietly. "Now let me tell you what to expect from me." He cups my jaw. "At this stage, I will always tell you what's coming before it happens. No surprises. No pushing you into things you're not ready for. As we build trust, that might shift—but right now, you'll know what to expect before we do anything."

I nod, a knot loosening in my chest.

"I expect honesty. Not pretending to like things to please me—that's not submission, that's performance. If you don't like something, you tell me. If you're scared, you tell me. My responsibility is your well-being, not your performance of pleasure."

"Okay," I whisper.

"And you need to understand—you have more power than you realize. You can stop anything, anytime. The safewords aren't decoration. Your limits are law."

"Now we establish the colors." His hand moves to my shoulder, fingers brushing against my pulse point. "Red means stop immediately. Yellow means slow down. Green means keep going. The tap signal still applies—if you can't speak but you need to tell me to stop, you tap me twice. Show me."

I tap his shoulder twice.

"Good girl."

The words detonate low in my belly. I'm wet and throbbing while learning consent protocols. This is absurd. And perfect.

We continue to talk. He asks about my history with men—which is sparse and disappointing—about pain, about what scares me, what I crave. His hand never stops moving, stroking my arm, my hair, the curve of my waist. When he asks about long-term plans, I'm honest.

"I want stability. Home and a family. People who stay."

His hand tightens on my hip. "My team—Tessa, Daniel, Cora—they're family to me. Home and family are important," he says quietly. "But I'd like a long-term submissive. We could see if this works out."

His thumb traces my lower belly. The touch sends electricity through me and makes me feel reckless.

"I trust you," I say. The words tumble out. "I'd give you—I'd do whatever you want."

His hands go still.

"Elise." There's a note in his voice I can't name. "Why do you trust me?"

"Because you've been careful. You've made sure I'm okay."

"That's why you should feel safe with me. I'm asking why you trust me. What's driving this? Are you saying you trust me because you're scared I'll leave if you don't?"

The words hit like a punch. "That's not—"

"Are you sure?" His thumb strokes my cheekbone. "If you're trying to earn me by giving me everything up front, and if you're trying to be perfect, to be easy, that's not submission, Elise. That's self-abandonment. And I won't let you do that, even for me."

Tears prick my eyes. "I don't know how to do this."

He presses his forehead to mine. "That's why we're talking before we go further. What we're doing is as much for me as it is for you. I asked you here because I want you—messy and uncertain, all of it."

The tears spill over, and I can't stop them. My voice cracks. "Then what do you want from me?"

"The truth. You're going to tell me one thing you're afraid of. One. Not everything. Not your whole history. One fear."

My throat is so tight I can barely breathe. I didn't expect to be sitting in his lap, revealing the deepest parts of myself. There's so much I'm afraid of.

I study his hand on my knee and pick my words carefully.

"I'm afraid that the moment I let myself need you, you'll realize I'm not worth the effort," I say softly. "The last time I let myself need someone, I was fourteen, and my foster mother told me I was 'just too much work' the week before I got moved again."

What I don't tell him is that I've never given a man the chance to say the same thing. I've walked away before they could reach the same conclusion. Why would Sebastian be any different?

He wraps his arms around me and pulls me fully against his chest.

"That's the beginning of trust. Not 'I'd do anything.' Not blind faith. You trusting me with your fear—that's what I want."

The dam breaks. All those years of holding it together and never needing anyone. Suddenly, I'm ugly crying. I can't remember the last time I let anyone see this. Maybe never.

He holds me and lets me fall apart in his lap without rushing me. His hand strokes my hair. The cotton of his shirt is soft against my cheek, damp now with my tears, and I can feel his heartbeat—steady, patient—beneath the fabric. My own breathing is ragged, hitching sobs that shake my whole body, but he doesn't flinch. Doesn't tell me to stop or ask what's wrong or try to fix it. He just holds me.

When the sobs finally slow, he pulls me closer. "How are you?"

"A mess." I let out a shaky laugh. "But good. I think."

"Good." His lips brush my temple.

We stay like that for a long time. Me curled in his lap, him holding me securely. The room is quiet except for our breathing.

Eventually, I become aware of his hardness pressing against my ass again. I shift slightly, and his breath catches.

"We're not done talking." His voice is rough. "But you're done listening, aren't you?"

My face flushes. My mind has drifted from negotiation to what his cock would feel like inside me.

"Yes."

He laughs softly. "Honest. I like that. But we're not doing anything else tonight. The anticipation is part of it, too."

I make a sound that's embarrassingly close to a whine. I've gone years without anyone touching me and survived just fine. Waiting shouldn't feel like torture, but here we are.

"Friday night," he says. "Two days from now. Be ready to use everything we discussed. The limits. The safewords. All of it."

Two days. Forty-eight hours of aching. Yep, I'm going to go crazy.

"And Elise?" His grasp tightens on my hip. "Don't touch yourself. The waiting is part of it. Two more days. You can do this."

My pussy clenches in protest. "That's cruel."

"That's the first test of your submission." His smile is wicked. "Consider it practice. Now, how did you get here tonight?"

"Subway."

"I'm calling you a car."

"Sebastian, that's not—"

"It wasn't a suggestion." His voice is gentle but firm. "You're not getting on public transit after tonight. Not like this."

Part of me wants to argue that I can take care of myself. But a bigger part, the part that's still floating somewhere soft and quiet, doesn't want to fight him on this. It feels good to be looked after.

"Okay."

He sends a quick text message. "Ten minutes."

He helps me to my feet, keeping one hand on my waist until he's certain I'm stable. He finds my shoes and kneels. I stare down at him as he slips them onto my feet. Holy fuck, this is hot.

"I want you to text me when you get home," he says, standing. "So I know you arrived safely."

"Okay."

"And if you feel like you are spiraling or need to hear my voice, you call me. I don't care what time it is."

A lump forms in my throat, and I nod.

He tips my chin up. "Remember. You're worth the effort."

He walks me to the elevator, and at the doors, he catches my wrist and turns me to face him.

"Friday night. I'm going to make you come until you forget your own name." His thumb finds my pulse point, presses gently. "And you're going to let me."

Heat pools between my thighs. "Yes."

"Yes, what?"

"Yes, Sir."

His eyes darken with satisfaction. Then I'm in the elevator and the doors are closing and I can still sense the warmth of his body against mine.

My phone buzzes before I reach the lobby.

Sebastian: You did well tonight. I'm proud of you.

I stare at the message until my vision blurs. He held me while I cried and made everything seem normal. He didn't flinch when I showed him my fear.

I'm in so much trouble.

Chapter 4

It's Friday. The night I've been waiting for is finally here. It's been forty-eight hours of not touching myself. Forty-eight hours of waking up wet from dreams I can't remember, my clit pulsing, and doing nothing about it because Sebastian Ashford told me not to.

Cold showers have become my religion. The cold water and I are in a committed relationship now. It's not going well. I keep cheating with hot water because I'm weak and apparently also a masochist who enjoys edging herself into insanity.

This is who I am now. A woman held hostage by her own arousal and a man who has been too busy to do more than smile and say hello as he passed my desk. The same man who texted me every night after work. Who told me he was looking forward to watching me fall apart on Friday.

But I haven't only been suffering these two days. I've been researching.

I've read BDSM articles and forums and first-person accounts until my eyes blurred. I've learned about negotiation and the difference between submission and surrender. The power exchange goes both ways. The submissive holds as much power as the dominant, maybe more. I choose what I give. I choose when I give it. And I can take it back whenever I want.

The woman who walked into Sebastian's office on Tuesday was uncertain. That woman is gone. Tonight, I'm going to get what I want.

His text last night instructed me to come to his office at five. My hair is pinned at the nape of my neck, and the exposed skin makes me hyperaware of every brush of air. I'm wearing a conservative blouse and a skirt that hits at the knee but is loose enough to be pulled up. I chose sensible heels. It's professional clothes for a woman who is absolutely not thinking about being bent over a desk.

Except I am. I've been wet since before my alarm went off. Since I opened my eyes and remembered that today, finally, I'm going to get his cock inside me. At least, I better get his cock inside me.

I feel like a grown woman pretending to be a functioning adult while my panties stick to me and my breasts ache. I've been counting down the minutes until five o'clock, and it's finally time.

Right before I get up, Lydia Kessler passes my desk, then pauses. "Working late again?" Her smile doesn't reach her eyes. "Dedication like that gets noticed."

Something about the way she says it makes my skin prickle. Is that a warning or a threat? I try to shake off thoughts of Lydia as I take the elevator up to the executive floor. I've got better things to think about.

When I get to Sebastian's office, my hands tremble as I knock. It's anticipation, not fear.

"Come in."

I push open the door and freeze. Sebastian stands by the windows, hands in his pockets. He doesn't turn when I enter, but I catch the shift in his stance. He knows it's me.

"Everyone's gone, but lock it."

He turns as the click echoes. His gaze travels down my body, and heat floods my cheeks. That look, like I'm already his. A hardness I haven't seen before sharpens his features, and my thighs press together on instinct. This is the dom.

"Come here."

My legs tremble as I cross the room. When I'm close enough to smell his cologne, a part of me wants to sink down. To wait for instruction. To be good.

Wait, fuck that.

I grab his shirt and pull him down toward me. "I'm done waiting."

The research taught me that submission isn't weakness. It's a gift I give when I choose to give it. And right now, I'm choosing to take instead.

His eyes flash. Surprise first, then heat so intense it steals my breath. His hands grip my hips hard enough to bruise. Good. I want the marks because I want proof this is real.

"Two days." I breathe the words against his mouth. "You made me wait two days. Do you have any idea how desperate I am right now?"

A rough sound escapes him. "Show me."

I grab his hand and shove it under my skirt, pressing it between my thighs. When his fingers push against the damp fabric of my panties, I whimper.

"Fuck." His voice is strained. "You're dripping."

"I told you." I rock against his hand without shame. "I've been like this for two days."

His free hand cups my jaw, tilting my face up. "I planned to talk first before anything happened tonight."

"No talking." I rub my palm along the hard ridge of his cock under his slacks. "Whatever you want to do to me tonight? The answer is yes."

His control wavers and I watch the careful mask crack.

"You don't know what I want to do to you."

"Then tell me."

"I want to tie you up. Bend you over my desk. I want to spank you until your ass is red, and then I want to fuck you until you have zero doubts that you're mine."

Lust slams into me, hollowing out my lungs. My pussy clenches around nothing.

"Yes." The word rips out of me. "God, yes. All of it."

"Say it properly." A muscle jumps in his jaw. He's holding himself in check. "Tell me exactly what you're consenting to."

My face burns, but I hold his gaze. "I want you to tie me up. Spank me. Fuck me until I can't think." I grip his shirt more tightly. "I want to be yours. Please, Sebastian. I need this."

He growls low in his throat. "If anything is too much—"

"Red to stop. Yellow to slow down. I remember." I'm practically vibrating with need. "Now give it to me."

The careful control in his expression hardens into pure command. "Strip."

My fingers tremble, but I don't hesitate. Blouse first, folded on the chair because he's watching and I want to be good. Skirt next. Bra.

Panties so wet the fabric peels away from me. His jaw tightens when he notices.

Goosebumps rise on my skin, and my nipples are painfully tight. I'm naked except for my heels, and right when I'm about to step out of them, he stops me.

"Keep the heels. I want to see you in nothing but those."

I straighten, naked except for four inches of black patent leather. His eyes darken with approval. "Perfect," he murmurs.

Then he reaches up and loosens his tie. Pulls it free from his collar in one smooth motion. The silk whispers against his shirt.

My breath catches. "Your tie?"

"We're improvising." He steps closer. "Color?"

"The greenest green that ever greened."

His mouth twitches. "Give me your hands."

I hold them out with wrists together. He binds them—wrapping the silk twice, knotting it with efficiency. Snug but not painful. The silk is smooth and cool against my skin, carrying his warmth. The pressure grounds me in a way I didn't expect.

This is what I needed, to stop making decisions and simply exist.

"Come."

He leads me to his massive desk and guides me forward until my hips press against the edge, then places one hand between my shoulder blades.

"Bend over."

I fold at the waist and stretch my bound hands across the cool surface. My cheek presses against the polished wood, and my ass is in the air while my pussy is exposed. He can see everything. All of me. Slick and swollen and desperate.

His palm traces over the curve of my ass, and I shiver.

"Ten. You're going to count each one out loud." His voice drops lower. "If you lose count, we start over from one. Understood?"

Ten. I can do ten. My pussy clenches in anticipation.

"Yes, Sir."

The first strike lands quickly.

Crack.

Sharp heat blooms across my right cheek. The sting radiates outward, transforming into warmth that arrows straight to my clit. It's a bright edge that makes me moan, but I wouldn't call it painful.

"One."

The second lands on my left. Harder. My skin heats, nerve endings sparking, and the hurt dissolves into pleasure so fast it steals my breath.

"Two."

He builds a rhythm. Each strike is an odd blend of pleasure and pain. By five, I'm panting. By seven, I'm whimpering as arousal coats my thighs.

"Eight." My voice breaks on the word.

He pauses. His palm soothes over heated skin, checking. "Color?"

"Green." I push my hips up. "Please. Keep going."

The ninth strike lands harder than the others. I cry out, and then my mind unlocks.

Not pain. The opposite. Permission. Every impact is permission to stop holding myself together. Three years of being invisible. Twenty-six years of being forgettable. Each strike says *you're here, you matter, I see you.*

"You're doing so well." His hand soothes over the heated curve of my ass. "Look at you. Taking everything I give you."

The praise hits harder than the spanking. My pussy clenches, and I moan, hips pressing against the edge of the desk, desperate for any friction.

"Nine," I manage.

The quiet settles inside me. Not the scared quiet I've lived with my whole life. This is different. Calm. Every decision taken out of my hands. I don't have to be perfect.

The final strike lands where my ass meets my thigh, and I cry out, arching off the desk.

"Ten." I'm soaked and shaking. I've never been this turned on in my entire life. My college self would be taking notes and telling me not to waste time with that TA.

He goes still behind me, and I glance over my shoulder. His eyes are dark, his breathing shallow. Controlled. Like he's managing a war I can't see.

This is what my submission costs him.

His eyes flutter closed for a heartbeat, a crack in the control, and when they open, there's rawness underneath. Not merely want. *Need.* The kind that mirrors mine.

He's not only doing this to me. I'm doing it to him too.

His fingers slide through my folds, and I make a noise that should embarrass me but doesn't.

"Dripping for me." His voice is rough. "Your body knows exactly who it belongs to."

"Yes, Sir." I face forward and push against his hand. "Please. I need—"

"I know what you need." I hear him step back. The clink of his belt. The rasp of his zipper. A condom wrapper tearing. The wait is almost unbearable, and then he runs the head of his cock through my folds.

I can't stop myself from begging. "Please fuck me. I need you inside me. *Now.*"

He grasps my hips and thrusts into me in one brutal stroke.

The stretch burns. Too much, perfectly too much. He's so deep I forget how to breathe. Forget my own name.

He withdraws, and the drag of him against my sensitive flesh makes me sob. He slams home again and hits a spot inside me that makes colors sparkle along the edges of my vision.

"Does this feel good?" His voice is strained. "I need to hear you."

"Full. So full." The words escape in fragments. "God, don't stop. Please don't stop."

He sets a punishing pace. Each thrust sends me deeper into a place I've never been. The pleasure builds in layers while I'm moaning with each collision against my sensitive ass. My thoughts dissolve.

"I could keep you like this." His voice is rough, every word punctuated by a thrust. "Every night. Spread open for me. *Mine.*"

My pussy clamps down so hard he curses.

"You like being claimed."

"Yes." The admission rips out of me. "I want to be yours. In every way."

He releases my hip and slides a hand up my spine to tangle his fingers in my hair. His control shatters. He drives into me harder, and I'm spiraling. So close. Right there.

"Come for me." His other hand snakes around to my clit, circling exactly where I need it. "Now."

I shatter. The orgasm rips through me, and I'm pulsing around him. The pleasure is too much. Not enough. Can't breathe. Can't think. Every nerve firing, cresting without end.

I'm sobbing his name and shaking so hard he has to hold me to the desk.

He fucks me through it. Each thrust extends the pleasure until I can't tell where one wave ends and the next begins. I'm flying apart and held together all at once.

His rhythm falters. He buries himself deep and comes with a guttural moan. Even through the condom, I imagine his warmth flooding me, and it triggers another aftershock.

When he stills, we're both breathing hard. Still connected.

My legs are useless. My brain is offline. For a moment, there's a blessed nothingness. Is this what heaven feels like?

"Elise." His voice is gentle now. "Still with me?"

"Mmm hmm," I manage. "Or maybe not. I'm dead now. This is my ghost speaking."

He gives a surprised laugh. When he pulls out carefully, I whimper at the loss. I hear him rustling with his clothes and watch him wrap the condom in tissue before tucking himself back into his slacks. He's putting away my new favorite toy. Rude. I wasn't finished with it.

He helps me stand, and my legs immediately prove they're more decorative than functional at the moment. Oops, guess I was done after all.

He steadies me against his desk and reaches for my bound wrists. His fingers are gentle as he works the silk free and massages where the tie left faint pink marks.

"Any numbness? Tingling?"

"No." I pause. "But my ass is tender. I blame you entirely."

He kisses each wrist, lips soft against the marks. Then he lifts me like I weigh nothing and carries me to the couch. When he settles with me in his lap, he wraps his arms around me.

I burrow into his warmth, feeling shy. Seems a little late now.

"Hey," he says gently. "Talk to me."

Suddenly, I'm crying. Oh god, he's going to think I'm nuts if I keep crying on him. I try to make light of it.

"I'm crying over good sex." A wet laugh escapes. "This is what my life has become. I'm a cliché, sobbing into the chest of my boss who spanked me over his desk."

"You're not a cliché." He pulls me closer. "You were wound up tight when you got here."

"Is this normal? The crying?"

"Completely." He strokes my hair. "I've got you, and you don't have to hold it together."

The permission to fall apart cracks me open. I sob against his chest while he holds me. His fingers working through my hair in slow, soothing strokes.

He reaches for a water bottle on the side table and tips it to my lips. "Drink."

The cold liquid helps, and gradually, the shaking and crying stop.

"I'm scared," I admit when I can speak again. "Of how much I want this."

He presses his forehead to mine. "That makes two of us."

He's scared too. The revelation settles into my chest. I thought I was alone in this free fall, but he's right here with me. Not that I know what to do with this knowledge. Everything is moving so fast.

We sit like that for a while, his hand in my hair, my head against his chest. The trembling fades into warmth.

Eventually, he helps me dress. He buttons my blouse and smooths my hair.

No one has ever taken care of me like this. The thought threatens to undo me all over again. Sebastian seems to understand what I need, even when I don't. Can this guy get any more amazing?

When I'm put together, he cups my face in his hands.

"I need to know. Are you okay? You aren't thinking of running?"

Now he's being crazy. With how much I want him? I look into his eyes. He really is scared too.

"No running."

Famous last words, probably. But for once, I want to see what happens if I let myself hope. Especially if what happens involves more desk-related activities.

His exhale carries relief. "Good. Because I'm not letting you go."

He walks me to his office door and before I leave, he pulls me into a slow, thorough kiss.

"Monday," he says against my lips. "After work, come to my condo."

"Yes, Sir."

His eyes darken. "Keep saying that, and I'm not letting you leave."

"Tempting." I give him my best cheeky smile. "But I should probably sleep at some point. My new boss is a demanding hardass."

"He definitely is." He opens the door. "Text me when you're home."

I barely remember the walk to the elevator, but once I'm inside, my phone buzzes.

Sebastian: You were perfect tonight.

Yep. Trouble with a capital T.

When I get home, I shower and eat dinner before crawling into bed. My ass is still warm. My pussy is still congratulating herself on her life choices. She has questionable judgment but excellent taste.

I replay everything. The sounds. The way he held me down. The way I begged for more and meant it. I'm basically a walking scandal at this point, and I've never been happier about anything in my life.

At nine, another text comes through.

Sebastian: One more thing.

I sit up in bed, pulse quickening.

Sebastian: Don't touch yourself until Monday night. I want you desperate when I see you again.

My mouth falls open. He wants me to wait three more days after what we did tonight. My clit is already throbbing again, and he wants me to ignore it for another seventy-two hours.

I should remind him that I'm a grown woman who can touch herself whenever she wants, but my thumbs type before my brain catches up.

Elise: Yes, Sir.

His response is immediate.

Sebastian: Good girl.

Heat floods through me. Yep, I'm a slut for my boss. It's going to be a long three days.

But for the first time in my life, I'm looking forward to the waiting.

Chapter 5

The weekend was torture, and it's finally Monday. Three days since Sebastian spanked me over his desk, fucked me until I forgot my own name, and then texted me with a rule specifically designed to make me insane. I white-knuckled my way through the entire weekend like a recovering addict. Took up stress baking. Burned two batches of cookies because I kept spacing out remembering the sound of his belt. My vibrator sat in my nightstand drawer, taunting me. I renamed it Judas because it can't help me now.

I'm so desperate I could cry.

I've been wet since I woke up this morning. Wet through my morning meeting. Wet through lunch with Cora, who cornered me at the sandwich counter and demanded we eat together because, quote, "you look like you're about to vibrate out of your skin and I need to know why."

She spends thirty minutes trying to crack me.

"You're glowing. It's disgusting." She stabs her salad with unnecessary violence. "Either you won the lottery or you're getting laid. Which is it?"

"Neither." I choke on my iced tea. "I'm just... focused. On work."

"Uh-huh." She narrows her eyes. "You know I can smell bullshit from three departments away, right? It's a very useful gift."

I survive by shoving food in my mouth and making noncommittal sounds until she gives up. Temporarily. The look she gives me when we part says *this isn't over*.

I'm also wet through my entire afternoon while Sebastian walks past my desk twice and doesn't even glance at me, the sadistic bastard.

Even an encounter with Lydia in the hallway doesn't dampen my anticipation. She gives me a too-sweet smile as we pass. "Settling into the new job?"

I mumble, "Yep," and keep walking. Three years here, and I don't know why she's now paying attention to me, but I'm too distracted by thoughts of Sebastian to worry about it.

His text arrives at three.

Sebastian: Tonight. 7. My condo.

Four hours. I count every minute. Squeezed my thighs together under my desk until Tessa asked if I needed to use the restroom. This is mortifying. I'm a professional woman reduced to a throbbing mess by a man who won't let me touch myself.

After work, when the elevator doors open directly into his condo, Sebastian is waiting. His sleeves are rolled to his elbows, and he looks relaxed. I want to murder him.

Also climb him like a tree. Conflicting urges.

"Elise." His voice wraps around my name, and my knees weaken. "Come in."

I step into his space. His world. His rules.

"Did you follow my instructions?"

Heat floods my cheeks. "Yes."

"Yes, what?"

"Yes, Sir." A shiver runs down my spine. "I didn't touch myself. Not once."

Does the water from my shower wand count? Nah...it's not like I orgasmed.

His eyes glitter with approval. "How do you feel?"

"Like I'm going to die if you don't put your hands on me in the next thirty seconds."

A slow smile spreads across his face. "That's exactly how I want you."

He doesn't touch me.

Not immediately. He guides me to the sectional with a hand that hovers at my lower spine without making contact. The almost-touch is worse than nothing. My skin tingles, desperate for friction.

"Sit."

I obey, and he sits beside me. He's close enough that I can smell his cologne, but we're not touching.

"Friday was our first formal scene." His voice is even. Calm. "I let your enthusiasm override my plans."

A tremor runs through me.

"I'm not complaining." His eyes hold mine. "But in the future, I'm going to be a little more strict." He leans back, studying me. "Tonight, we're going to do things properly. I want to show you how I build."

"Build to what?"

"To breaking you apart and putting you back together." He tilts his head, studying me. "You followed my rule for three days. You've proven you can wait. Now you're going to prove you can wait while I'm touching you."

Oh fuck. "You're going to edge me."

"I'm going to take you to the edge and hold you there until I decide you've earned release." He leans closer. "Color?"

"Green." The word comes out rough. "Very, very green."

"Stand."

I rise on shaking legs. Somewhere, an HR manual is spontaneously combusting. A workplace safety poster is weeping. I'm about to let my boss edge me until I lose the ability to form coherent thought, and the only thing I'm worried about is whether I'll cry before or after I start begging.

Probably during. Let's be honest.

"I'm going to undress you first, and then I'm going to bind your wrists. You're going to watch everything I'm doing."

His fingers move to my blouse. One button. Two. By the time the fabric falls open, I'm trembling.

Bra. Skirt. Panties. Heels. Each piece is removed with care, folded, and set aside. When I'm naked, he produces silk rope from a drawer in a side table.

"This is formal restraint. Prepared materials, not improvised. I want you to understand the difference."

"The difference being?"

"My tie was spontaneous." He steps closer. "This means I planned for it. Wanted it."

Heat blooms low in my belly. "I want that too."

"Hold out your hands."

My wrists press together. He loops the rope around them, and the silk tightens, snug against my skin.

"Pull against it."

I tug and it gives slightly but doesn't release.

"Can you feel your fingers? Wiggle them for me."

I flex my fingers.

"Any tingling? Numbness?"

"No."

"Good. That's the right tension. Secure enough to remind you that you can't fidget." His thumb traces over the silk.

A different kind of quiet settles over me. I can't twist my fingers easily or tap my nails or do any of the little movements that let me escape my own skin.

He guides me to the couch and positions me bent over the arm, my bound wrists stretched in front of me.

"We start with impact. I'm going to show you how I warm up to bring blood to the surface. It changes how the real strikes land. I'll do fifteen."

He rests his hand on my skin and traces soothing circles before starting with light, quick pats that tingle more than sting. He covers my entire ass, alternating cheeks, building heat gradually.

"Notice the difference?"

"Yes, Sir." My voice is already breathy as the anticipation coils tight in my belly.

"Now you count." The first real strike lands.

Heat blooms across my right cheek. Sharper than the warm-up, but the earlier attention softens the blow. The sting radiates outward, transforming into delight that pulses directly to my clit.

"One."

The second lands on my left. Harder. My hips jerk forward.

"Two."

By five, the impact stings and leaves a throbbing warmth behind. My pussy clenches around nothing.

"Five." The word comes out breathless.

His hand traces over the heated flesh. "Color?"

"Mmm, green."

The next five come faster. Each strike makes my thoughts scatter. The spreadsheets, the meetings, the constant narration in my head: gone. There's only his hand and my counting and the pleasure spreading through my body.

"Ten."

His hand fists in my hair and tugs. Not hard enough to hurt, but enough to arch my spine and expose my throat.

"You're doing so well." His voice is rough against my ear. "Five more. Then we move to the real lesson."

The last five blend together. Each spank is sharper than the last. His hand in my hair keeps me arched. By fifteen, I'm shaking and desperate.

"Fifteen." My voice cracks on the word.

He releases my hair and helps me stand on trembling legs. Then I'm on my back on the couch, bound wrists above my head, hooked to an anchor point I definitely didn't notice last time.

To be fair, last time I was sobbing into his shoulder. Not exactly scanning the wall for bondage hardware. This couch has seen two very different sides of me now. Emotional wreck and willing captive. I'm a versatile guest.

"Now." He kneels beside the couch, positioning himself at my hip. "Now we see how well you can wait. Spread your legs for me."

I do. Wide. Shameless. Three days of denial have stripped away every pretense of modesty.

He runs one finger from my navel down to the top of my mound. Stops there. Doesn't go lower.

"Please." The word escapes before I can catch it.

"Please what?"

"Touch me. I need—"

"I am touching you." His finger traces a lazy circle. "Be specific."

My face burns. "My clit. Touch my clit. Please, Sir."

"Since you asked so nicely."

Oh, thank you, Jebus. Reduced to begging in minutes. Judas the vibrator could never.

His finger slides lower and parts my folds. He finds the swollen bundle of nerves that's been aching for three days.

The first touch makes me cry out as my hips jerk off the couch. Three days of deprivation have left me so sensitive that one brush of his finger sends lightning through my nervous system.

His voice is rough. "You really did follow my rule."

"Told you," I pant and roll my hips.

He plays with me like an instrument. Two fingers sliding through my folds, spreading the slickness, circling my clit. The pleasure builds in waves. I'm already so close.

His hand withdraws.

"No!" The word rips out of me. My hips chase his retreating fingers. They have their own agenda now. Their agenda was not approved by management. "Sebastian—"

"You were about to come." Not a question. "I could feel it."

"Yes. I was so close—"

"And you'll get there again when I decide." His hand returns to my thigh, stroking gently. That's not where I need him. "That's the first edge. Three more, and then you can have what you want."

"Three more?" I might actually cry. I've become a person who weeps over denied orgasms. "I can't."

"You can, and you will." His fingers find my clit again. "Because I'm telling you to."

He builds me up again. More slowly this time. Two fingers slide inside me while his thumb works my clit, and the stretch makes me moan. He curls his fingers, finds a spot that makes my vision white out.

"There." There's satisfaction in his voice. "Found it."

He strokes that spot ruthlessly. The pleasure builds faster, sharper, and I'm right there, right on the edge.

His hand stops and holds still inside me without moving.

I sob. Actually sob. Real tears leak down my temples into my hair. Very sexy. Very dignified. My pussy clenches around his fingers, desperate for more.

"Color?" His voice is strained.

"Green," I manage. "I hate you, but green."

He laughs. "No, you don't."

He's right. I don't.

The third edge is worse. He uses his mouth.

One moment, he's kneeling beside me. The next, he's shifting between my spread thighs, his shoulders pushing my legs wider, and then his mouth is on me and I scream.

His tongue drags through my folds. Hot and wet and devastatingly slow.

I make a sound I've never heard from my own throat. Not a moan. Not a word. Something animal.

"Oh God, Sebastian."

He pulls back just enough to speak against my pussy, the vibration of his words making me shake. "You taste incredible. I've been thinking about this for days." His tongue circles my entrance. "About spreading you open and making you squirm."

My bound hands tug uselessly above my head. I can only lie here and take whatever he gives me.

His tongue traces patterns I can't predict. Broad strokes that flatten against my clit, then pointed flicks that have me arching off the couch. He alternates pressure and speed, until I'm writhing and coherent thought becomes impossible.

"Please," I whimper. "I need—"

"I know what you need." He sucks my clit into his mouth, and the suction is so perfect I nearly shatter right there. His tongue works against me, and the sensation...

He releases me and pulls away. I'm gasping while my pussy throbs with denied release.

"No, no, no—" There's no shame left. "Please, I was so close, please let me come."

"One more." He presses a kiss to my inner thigh, his stubble scraping the sensitive skin. "You're doing so well. One more, and then I'll give you everything."

Tears leak from the corners of my eyes. "I can't. I can't—"

"You can." He kisses my other thigh. "Because you're mine. And I'm telling you that you can."

The fourth edge breaks me open.

He uses everything. Two fingers slide inside me, curling against that spot he found earlier. His mouth returns to my clit, tongue circling in relentless patterns. His free hand grips my hip, holding me still when I try to writhe away from the intensity.

This time there's no teasing. He's relentless.

His fingers pump into me while his tongue works my clit. He finds a rhythm, thrust and suck. He circles and repeats, holding me there as the pleasure builds like a wave gathering force.

"That's it." His voice is rough against my pussy, the words vibrating through me. "That's my good girl. Feel how badly you need to come."

I can't respond. The pleasure consumes every thought, every cell, every atom of my being. My legs shake. My bound hands twist against the silk. I'm going to shatter into pieces and never reassemble.

"I can feel you clenching around my fingers." He thrusts deeper, hits that spot harder. "So tight. So desperate. You want to come so badly, don't you?"

"Yes. Yes. Yes. Yes."

He sucks my clit hard, and I'm right there, right at the edge, one more second, and I'll explode.

The world goes soft. The constant narration in my head, the criticism, the worry: gone. There's only his mouth and his hands and the pleasure that keeps climbing without cresting.

I'm floating. Time stretches. Everything goes quiet.

"Such a good girl." His voice reaches me from somewhere far away.

"Please, let me come," I whimper.

"Come." His tongue circles my clit one final time. "Now."

The orgasm doesn't crest. It detonates.

Three days of denial and four edges of torment explode outward from my core. My spine arches off the couch. I scream his name. My pussy pulses around his fingers while his mouth continues to work my clit, drawing out the pleasure until I can't tell where one wave ends and the next begins.

His fingers keep thrusting, hitting that spot inside me over and over. His tongue keeps circling, keeps flicking, keeps driving me higher. The first orgasm bleeds into a second, or maybe it's just one that refuses to end. I'm sobbing and shaking and coming apart so completely that I forget I have a body at all.

When it finally ebbs, I'm boneless. Floating. The world is cotton and warmth and distant sounds.

Sebastian moves. I register it remotely. He's untying my wrists and massaging where the silk left marks before pulling me into his arms.

"You did so well. So fucking perfect for me." His voice is tender and not the commanding tone he used during the scene.

I try to speak but can't form words. I only manage a sound that might be his name.

"Don't try to talk yet." He strokes my hair. "This is what your brain does when you let go completely. The words will come back."

I burrow into his chest. He's still clothed. I'm naked. The imbalance should bother me, but nothing bothers me. I'm floating and safe and held.

Time moves strangely.

At some point, a blanket appears around my shoulders. Water presses to my lips. Sebastian's voice murmurs praise I can't quite parse but that settles warm in my chest anyway.

The floating recedes gradually, like waking from a deep sleep. I become aware of my body again and the pleasant ache between my thighs. My ass is warm from the spanking, and there's faint marks on my wrists from the rope. Sebastian's heartbeat is steady under my cheek.

"Welcome back." He kisses my temple. "How do you feel?"

"Like I don't have bones." My words slur slightly. "Like I'm made of honey."

He laughs softly. "That's subspace. Your brain releases chemicals when you surrender like that. It's a reward for letting go."

"Is it always like this?"

His arm tightens around me. "Sometimes. It's a little different for everyone."

"I didn't know it could be like this." My throat tightens. "I didn't know I could be like this."

"You've always had this inside you." He presses another kiss to my hair. "You were waiting for someone safe to show it to."

The tears come then. It's not from sadness or pain but from the sheer relief of being seen and held. From being wanted exactly as I am.

He holds me through the tears, not trying to fix them. When they finally stop, exhaustion pulls at me.

"Stay tonight." His voice is soft. It's not a command.

"Okay," I whisper. "I'd like that."

He carries me to his bedroom and lays me in sheets that smell like him before he climbs in beside me and pulls me against his chest.

For the first time in my life, the voice in my head is silent as I fall asleep.

CHAPTER 6

The bed is empty when I wake up.

My hand reaches across cool sheets before my brain catches up. Panic surges, instant and familiar. He left. Of course he left. Last night was too much, I was too much, he saw all of me and decided I wasn't worth staying for.

The clatter of dishes from somewhere beyond the bedroom stops the spiral.

I sit up, blink at the room I barely registered last night. High ceilings. Gray walls. A dresser with a single framed photo I can't make out from here. Everything is clean and orderly, except for me. I'm a mess of tangled hair, and I'm betting my mascara is smudged. I'm pretty sure a hickey is blooming on my collarbone.

Right. He carried me to bed.

Another clatter. Then the smell of coffee.

One of his shirts is draped over a chair by the window. He must have set it out while I slept. The cotton is soft when I pull it on, still carrying the faint scent of his cologne. It falls to mid-thigh and makes me feel deliciously claimed.

I clean up in the bathroom, and when I walk into the kitchen, Sebastian is at the stove in sweatpants and nothing else. His shoulders shift as he moves a pan. The muscles in his spine flex. His hair is disheveled, and there's a softness to him I've never seen before. This is what he looks like unguarded.

He turns before I announce myself. "Morning."

"You cook."

"I do a lot of things." He gives me a half-smile. "Sit and drink your coffee. The eggs will be ready in a minute."

He has a mug waiting for me on the counter. I take it to the table with me and wrap my hands around it. When I take a sip, I groan in appreciation. He added the perfect amount of cream.

"How did you know?"

He understands what I'm asking. "I pay attention." He plates the eggs and slides them in front of me. "Eat."

It's so easy to let him take care of me like this. We chat while we eat. He asks about my schedule. I ask about his. Normal morning conversation, except I'm wearing his shirt and nothing else, and every time our eyes meet, I remember what his tongue felt like against my clit.

"Shower?" He stands and collects our plates. "We should leave in an hour."

"We?"

"We'll ride together to work." His tone brooks no argument.

We shower together. His hands work shampoo through my hair, fingers gentle at my scalp. The intimacy of it feels almost more exposing than anything from last night. Steam rises around us and water streams down his chest. I trace the lines of muscle with my fingertips, and he catches my hand, presses a kiss to my palm.

"If we start that, we'll never make it to the office."

"Would that be so bad?"

"Yes." But he's smiling. "Some of us have quarterly meetings."

He washes me tenderly. His hands are careful around the still-sensitive spots. When we step out, he wraps me in a towel and kisses my forehead like I'm precious.

I could get used to this. That thought should scare me more than it does.

The car he calls idles at the curb. Sebastian opens the back door for me, then slides in beside me. The partition is up, giving us privacy.

His hand finds my knee as the city slides past the tinted windows. A simple touch. A reminder that I'm his.

We pull up to the building, and he releases my knee. Professional distance snapping into place like a switch being thrown. When he opens my door, his expression is neutral. Controlled.

"Have a good day, Ms. Hart."

"You too, Mr. Ashford."

His eyes flicker with amusement before he turns and walks toward the executive entrance. I watch him go, trying to reconcile the man who just washed my hair with the CEO whose stride parts the crowd in the lobby.

I'm addicted to every version of him.

The quarterly meeting drags into its second hour. Sebastian sits at the head of the conference table. I'm sitting three seats away from him and he's in full CEO mode. He hasn't looked at me once.

My brain knows this is necessary. The professional and personal divide matters. He can't spend meetings staring at the woman he made come harder than she's ever come in her life.

My insecurities don't care what my brain knows.

Lydia Kessler sits near the front, taking notes with the dedication of someone building a case. Twice during Daniel's presentation, her gaze slides toward me. It's not hostile, but my skin prickles with awareness.

I force myself to focus on the projections. Revenue margins. Integration timelines. Numbers that should matter more than whether Sebastian will look at me.

My phone buzzes against my thigh and I glance down.

Sebastian: You're fidgeting. Stop.

My hands freeze and I look up at him suspiciously.

His attention is fixed on the projector screen, and his phone rests on the table. Was he even looking when he typed that?

A minute later, there's another text.

Sebastian: Good girl.

My thighs clench under the table. A flush crawls up my neck, and I have to focus very hard on breathing normally while Daniel explains vendor consolidation.

The entire team is here taking notes, asking questions, checking their phones. Cora's in the corner, scribbling furiously on her notepad like she's transcribing for posterity. She catches my eye and angles the page my way. It's a tiny screaming face with the word *HELP* underneath. I nearly choke.

None of them sees the electricity arcing between us. None of them knows Sebastian just made me wet in the middle of the meeting.

The secret is intoxicating.

Lydia's eyes find mine across the table. Something flickers in her expression. Recognition? Suspicion?

Okay, maybe she senses something. I hold her gaze until she looks away.

The break room is usually empty at two. Everyone's in post-lunch meetings or buried in work. The perfect time to splash cold water on my face and collect myself.

Cora's leaving as I approach, coffee in hand, laptop tucked under her arm.

"Hey." She pauses in the doorway. "Your presentation last week? The retention model? Sebastian sent it to the department heads."

I blink. "He did?"

"Mm-hmm. I heard two of them fighting over who gets to claim they mentored you." She grins. "You're making enemies in high places. I'm proud."

She's gone before I can process that, leaving me standing in the doorway like an idiot.

Tessa's getting coffee when I walk into the break room. She glances up and her eyes sharpen. The collar of my blouse suddenly feels too high, even though the marks Sebastian left are well hidden.

"Long meeting?" she asks.

"That obvious?"

She pours me a cup of coffee without asking and slides it toward me. "Sebastian runs hot and cold professionally. Don't let it throw you."

My hand pauses before I lift the mug. "I'm sorry?"

"In meetings, he's all business. It can make you feel invisible." She sips her coffee. "But that's not who he is. It's how he compartmentalizes. Don't mistake his work mode for his real self."

The advice is too pointed to be a coincidence.

"You know him well?" I ask carefully.

"I know the type." Her smile is warm. "You've got the look, you know. The floaty one. Seth—my husband—calls it 'the glow.' Says I get it after a good scene."

My face flames. "I don't—"

"Relax." She sets down her cup, and her expression softens into something like understanding. "Fifteen years of marriage to a dom. I know the look because I wear it too."

I don't know what to say. She's telling me she understands. I'm not alone. Whatever I'm discovering with Sebastian isn't shameful or strange.

"If you ever need to talk about anything," Tessa says quietly, "I'm here. No judgment." A pause. "I've been where you are. Someone helped me understand it wasn't weakness. Consider this me paying it forward."

She leaves before I can respond.

I stand there, coffee cooling in my hands. Someone sees me and doesn't think I'm broken.

It's 4:47 and I'm pretending to review the Catalyst project files when my phone buzzes.

Sebastian: I have something new to show you tonight.

My thighs clench under my desk. The anticipation that's been simmering all day spikes into something sharper. Needier.

Elise: What kind of something?

Sebastian: The kind you'll understand when you experience it.

Elise: That's inconceivable.

Sebastian: Princess Bride. Cute. And you keep using that word...

Elise: I know exactly what it means. I still want to know.

Sebastian: Come to my place at 7. Not a minute later.

I bite my lip to keep from grinning at my screen like an idiot. The CEO of my company is flirting with me via text, and I'm quoting rom-coms at him. This is either the beginning of the best thing that's ever happened to me, or a spectacular disaster waiting to unfold.

Probably both.

Elise: Fine. 7.

Sebastian: Wear something easy to remove.

Heat rushes through me so quickly I have to set down my phone. Across the floor, Lydia Kessler is watching me. Her expression is unreadable, but just the fact she's paying attention to me makes me uneasy.

I pull up a spreadsheet and force myself to look busy. Like I'm not counting down the minutes until I can kneel at Sebastian Ashford's feet and let him do unspeakable things to my body.

Two hours and thirteen minutes.

I can be patient.

Sure, I'll get right on that.

CHAPTER 7

The elevator opens, and my heart trips.

Forty-five minutes. That's how long I spent choosing this dress, a wrap style in deep green that ties at the side. Easy access. Exactly what he asked for. Underneath, black lace bra and panties that will probably be on his floor in minutes.

Sebastian waits in the living room, and the sight of him steals my breath. He's in jeans and a t-shirt. He's devastating in a suit, but this is the man beneath the CEO. The one who texts me instructions about what to wear and where to be.

The one who's been living rent-free in my head all day while I pretended to focus on spreadsheets.

He doesn't greet me with words. His gaze travels down my body slowly, and the appreciation in his eyes sends a zing straight to my core.

"You followed instructions. This color suits you."

"I hoped you'd like it."

"I do." His palm settles at my waist, warm through the fabric. My breath hitches. "Come with me."

He leads me to his bedroom. To the bed that dominates the room. The bed where I've imagined him doing unspeakably dirty things to me during boring meetings.

Very professional, Elise. Your quarterly review is going to be interesting.

"Stand there." He points to a spot at the foot of the bed. "Don't move."

Then he circles me. His gaze is a physical weight. My nipples tighten, and I fight the urge to press my thighs together. I can already feel how slick they are.

I hold still because I want to please him. It's crazy how much I want to hear him call me a good girl.

"I've been thinking about this all day." His voice is low behind me, and it makes my spine liquid. "About unwrapping you."

His fingers find the tie at my waist. One slow pull, and the dress falls open, slides off my shoulders. The cool air hits my skin. I'm standing in his bedroom in black lace and nothing else. The woman I was a month ago would be having a panic attack.

Current me? Current me is wet and aching and pathetically grateful that he wants to unwrap me at all.

"Beautiful." He traces the edge of my bra with one finger, light enough to make me shiver. "But these need to go."

When he releases the clasp, the lace falls away and he cups my breasts. His thumbs brush over my nipples, and I gasp—high and needy and embarrassingly desperate.

His fingers hook into the waistband of my panties. "These too."

He drags the lace down my thighs, and I step out of them, leaving me completely naked as a flush spreads across my chest.

"On the bed. Face up. Arms above your head."

I crawl onto the mattress, position myself where he indicated. The buttery soft sheets are cool against my overheated skin.

When I stretch my arms overhead, my fingers brush the headboard.

Sebastian moves to the side of the bed and reaches beneath the mattress near the headboard. I hear a soft click, and he pulls out a padded cuff from where it was hidden behind the bed frame.

My eyes widen and my breath stutters.

"I installed this last week. Built-in restraints. No visible hardware."

He installed restraints in his bed. For me. He was thinking about tying me up while I was probably stress-eating granola bars at my desk and wondering if he was tired of me yet.

The cuff closes around my left wrist, soft padding against my skin. When I pull experimentally, it doesn't give.

Oh.

Oh.

A flood of heat pools between my legs. My rational brain goes very, very quiet.

"And your ankles." He moves to the foot of the bed, reaching beneath to release two more cuffs. His eyes find mine. "Spread open."

"Yes." The word comes out steady even though my heart is trying to escape through my ribs.

"Exposed. Completely vulnerable." He says it like he's reading from my internal monologue.

"Color?"

"Green." No hesitation. I'm thrilled and turned on, and my pussy is apparently running this show now. She's decided vulnerability is *hot*.

My right ankle is bound. He tests the restraint, checking tension, sliding a finger beneath the padding to verify circulation. Then he secures my right wrist.

The position he creates is obscene. Wrists above my head, legs spread wide. I can't hide any part of myself from his gaze. My pussy is already dripping and aching. He can clearly see how desperate I am for him.

This is what you wanted, some honest part of me admits. *This is what you've fantasized about while pretending to be a functional adult.*

"Look at you." His voice drops lower. "Waiting for whatever I want to do to you."

The vulnerability crashes over me like a wave. I'm helpless here, spread open and defenseless and entirely at his mercy.

And the realization doesn't frighten me.

It *ignites* me.

"Please."

So much for dignity.

"Please what?"

"Fuck me." I have no shame. "I've been waiting all day."

He smirks, clearly pleased at how desperate I am. "I know you have."

His hands trace patterns across my skin. My collarbone, the curve of my ribs, the soft plane of my stomach. Everywhere except my breasts. Everywhere except my throbbing pussy.

This is how I die. Death by delayed gratification. They'll put it on my tombstone: *She waited for Sebastian Ashford to touch her pussy and her heart gave out.*

"Sebastian," I whine and rock my hips.

"Patience." He trails one finger through my folds, gathering the slickness. "You're already soaked."

Heat floods my face. He didn't need to point it out. The evidence is glistening on my inner thighs.

"Ask me nicely," he says. "Tell me what you want."

"Rub my pussy. Please, Sir."

His thumb traces through my folds again, maddeningly light. "You think you deserve it?"

"Yes." I arch into his touch as much as the restraints allow—which isn't much. "I've been good. I need you."

I hope he doesn't ask what I've done to be good. I wouldn't be able to think of a single thing right now, other than I haven't been touching myself without him.

"I know what you need."

He strips efficiently. Shirt first, revealing the chest I love to run my fingers over in the shower. Jeans and boxer briefs are pulled off together. His cock looks thicker than before, and I moan when I notice the glistening tip.

My mouth waters. Literally waters at the sight of his dick. I've definitely boarded the slut train and bought a one-way ticket for this man.

He rolls on a condom with steady hands. The anticipation coils more tightly in my core, watching him, knowing what comes next, unable to speed it up or slow it down.

He climbs onto the bed and settles between my spread thighs. The heat of his body radiates against my oversensitized skin. His cock brushes my entrance, and I make an inhuman sound. Half moan, maybe a prayer spoken in tongues.

"Eyes on me. I want to watch you when I take what's mine."

What's mine.

The possessiveness thrills me, and I moan as he pushes inside slowly, inch by inch, until he bottoms out.

"Ooooh, god." I toss my head from side to side and try to rock against him to get him to fuck me.

I'm going to go insane.

"That's it." His voice is strained, like control is costing him. "Your pussy is gripping me like it was made for me."

I can't answer. Can't form words. My wrists strain against the cuffs because I want to pull him closer, but I *can't*.

He fucks me with long strokes that drag against every sensitive spot. My hips try to rise to meet him, but the ankle restraints limit my movement. All I can do is lie here and take what he gives me.

Take what he gives me.

The thought alone nearly undoes me.

"I imagined this moment." He thrusts harder. "About you tied up in my bed. Spread open for me." Another thrust, deep enough to make me cry out. "I could keep you like this all the time."

My pussy clenches around him, and I'm fairly certain my brain short-circuits.

"Spread open. Waiting for me to fill you up." He grinds against me, hitting that spot inside that makes my vision blur. "Desperate for my cum. Begging for another load."

The mental image hits me like a truck. Me. Here. Filled and leaking and desperate for another round. I didn't know I wanted that, but my clit throbs like it's the best idea he's ever had.

What is happening right now?

"You liked that." His eyes are locked on my face. "Your pussy tightened when I said it."

I can't deny it. The evidence is clenching around his cock in rhythmic pulses, giving me away completely.

"Yes," I whisper.

His expression shifts. Darker. More intent.

"You'd take everything I gave you, wouldn't you?" He picks up the pace, fucking into me harder. "Every drop."

"God, yes." The words come out broken. Beyond my control.

"Imagine me filling you. *Really* filling you." He drives deep, holds there, grinds against my clit until I'm whimpering. "No condom. Nothing between us. Just me pumping you full of cum over and over again."

The image detonates in my mind.

Sebastian's bare cock inside me. His cum flooding my pussy with nothing to stop him from getting me pregnant.

Fuck. A shiver of delight ripples from my head to my toes, and I buck against him.

"Sebastian." My voice breaks on his name. "Oh god, Sebastian."

He pulls almost completely out, then slams home. "Look at that. The thought of me breeding you makes you clench like a fist."

Breed.

The word crashes through me, and my body responds without my permission: pussy gripping tight, hips straining against the restraints, desperate sounds spilling from my throat.

This is so messed up, but I don't care. I want to be his cumdumpster that he leaves tied to the bed. He can visit me to unload. I'll just be cumdrunk and happy until he gets me pregnant.

He fucks me faster, driven by his own need building in his expression. "I'm going to fill this perfect pussy until it's dripping down your thighs."

"Oooh, god!"

Another brutal thrust, and I explode. The orgasm tears through me like nothing I've experienced. My pussy spasms around his cock, and I'm crying out nonsense, pulling against the restraints. The pleasure goes on and on, wave after wave, intensified by the helplessness of my position.

He follows me over the edge with a guttural groan, burying himself deep as his cock pulses inside me. Through the haze of my climax, I imagine I really can feel the heat of his cum through the condom.

I wish he'd take the condom off.

The thought shocks me, even though it's true.

When the aftershocks finally fade, he's staring down at me with a fierce tenderness before he kisses me gently.

"Are you okay?"

Uh...I don't think he wants to know I was imagining him knocking me up, so I murmur, "Mmm, yes. So good."

He releases my ankles first. His hands are gentle as he works the cuffs open, checking the skin beneath for marks. A faint pink line circles each ankle where I strained against the padding. He presses his lips to each one softly before moving to my wrists.

"Any numbness?" He massages my left wrist, his thumbs working small circles into my palm.

"No." My voice is hoarse. "A little sore."

"You pulled hard when you came." He switches to my right wrist, giving it the same careful attention.

The reminder sends an aftershock zipping through me. I pulled hard because I was imagining him filling me with cum and getting me pregnant.

When I'm freed, he settles with his head against the pillows and pulls me into his arms. I rest against his chest, listening to his steady heartbeat. Mine slows down to match his.

For a long moment, neither of us speaks. His fingers trace lazy patterns on my spine while my brain tries to reboot.

So. Breeding kink. That's apparently a thing I have now. Cool. Cool cool cool.

"Was the breeding dirty talk okay?" His voice is careful. His hand stills on my spine, and when I lift my head, his eyes are watchful. Waiting.

Warmth blooms in my chest, and a flush creeps up my neck. "Yes. I liked it. What you said."

Understatement of the century. My pussy has donned a reflective vest and is waving light wands, ready to guide his sperm straight to my eggs. *This way, gentlemen. Right this way.*

"Yeah?" He brushes a strand of hair from my face.

"You could..." I'm blushing so hard I'm surprised the room isn't glowing. "If you wanted to. Keep talking. Like that."

The rumble of his laugh vibrates through his chest, and I love the sound of it. Love that I'm one of the people who gets to hear it.

"Noted." His voice drops lower. "And seeing you react like that? How hard you came." His hand slides down my spine and rests on my ass. "I'm absolutely going to keep doing it."

My pussy spasms in anticipation, and I tuck my head under his chin and nuzzle closer into his warmth. I'm not sure this man could get any more incredible.

His arm tightens around me. "Now sleep."

"Bossy."

"You like it."

I do. God help me, I do.

The room smells like him and sex, and his arm is a warm weight across my waist. The hamster wheel of anxiety that usually spins in my head is quiet. Wrapped up in him like this, the world outside feels very far away.

Don't get used to this, the scared part of me whispers. *Good things don't last. People don't stay.*

But his arm tightens, and his breathing evens out, and my brain—for once—decides to shut up.

Sleep drags me under.

I wake to dim morning light filtering through the curtains and Sebastian's cock pressed against my ass.

Hard. Insistent. Impatient.

"Morning." His voice is rough with sleep, and he slides his hand up to cup my breast, thumb circling my nipple until it peaks.

"Is this your version of an alarm clock?" I'm aiming for teasing, but I just sound breathless and turned on.

"I like you soft and sleepy in the morning." His teeth graze my earlobe, and I shudder. "Before your brain starts running through all the reasons you shouldn't be here."

Rude. Accurate, but rude.

Still half-asleep. Already wet. This is my life now.

"We'll be late for our morning meeting," I protest weakly.

"I'm the boss." He rolls me onto my stomach, settling his weight over me, and the press of his body drives every coherent thought from my head. "I decide when meetings start."

His cock notches at my entrance, and I stop caring about schedules entirely.

Whatever. Work can wait.

CHAPTER 8

We're not late to the meeting. Thank God. Because there's a new face at the table, and I'd rather not give her any ammunition.

Not new to the company, since Lydia Kessler has been Senior Director for six years, but new to the integration meetings. Now she's sitting three chairs from where I'm presenting and watching me with the kind of focus that makes my skin prickle.

Daniel mentioned she pushed to be included. "Cross-departmental oversight," she'd called it.

Translation: I smell blood in the water, and I want a front row seat.

My palms are sweating. I wipe them on my skirt under the table and pull up my first slide.

"The retention model accounts for variables the previous analysis overlooked." It's a miracle that my voice is steady. "If we implement the phased approach, we can reduce attrition by eighteen percent in the first quarter alone."

"Interesting." Lydia's voice slices through the room. She's immaculate in cream silk, not a hair out of place, and her smile doesn't reach her eyes. "I'm curious how someone at your level arrived at these projections. The senior team spent months on integration strategy."

Translation: Who the fuck do you think you are?

Heat crawls up my neck. My mouth opens—

"Elise's model identified a twelve percent revenue gap that the senior team missed entirely." Sebastian's voice is ice. He hasn't looked at Lydia, but the temperature in the room drops. "Her analysis has already been validated by three department heads. Continue, Elise."

I click to the next slide, but my brain is doing that thing where it splits in two. Half of me wants to melt into a puddle of gratitude. The other half is screaming danger, danger, he just defended you publicly, she's going to use this.

Lydia's smile doesn't waver. Her eyes track me for the rest of the presentation. Every glance makes my shoulders tighten. This isn't good.

After the meeting, she catches me in the hallway.

"Impressive work." Her tone is pleasant. Her expression is anything but. "Sebastian seems quite...invested in your success."

"He's invested in results." I keep my voice neutral, which deserves some kind of award because my heart is trying to escape through my throat. "The projections speak for themselves."

"I'm sure they do." She tilts her head, studying me. "It's just interesting, isn't it? How quickly you've risen. Some people might wonder what else you're bringing to the table."

The implication lands like a slap. She doesn't know. She can't know. I thought we'd been careful. But heat floods my face like a confession.

Before I can respond, Tessa appears at my elbow. "Elise, Sebastian needs the revised numbers for the Thornton file. Now, if you don't mind."

Lydia's smile sharpens. "Of course. We'll continue this conversation later."

She walks away, heels clicking against marble.

"Ignore her." Tessa steers me toward the elevator.

"She thinks I'm sleeping my way to the top."

"She probably thinks everyone is sleeping their way somewhere. It's how her brain works." Tessa jabs the elevator button. "Don't let her get in your head. You earned your position. Everyone who matters knows it."

I try to shake it off, but Lydia's words cling to me.

What else you're bringing to the table.

She doesn't know anything. She's fishing.

I hope.

Thursday night. Seven o'clock.

Sebastian's text from an hour ago sits on my phone.

Sebastian: When you arrive, remove your shoes at the door. Kneel. Wait for me.

I spent all of yesterday replaying Lydia's words until my brain felt like static. But his text cut through the noise. Clear and simple. Do this. Nothing else matters.

The elevator opens into his condo, and I step inside. My heart is pounding because tonight is different. He instructed me to take off my shoes and kneel in the entryway and wait for him. I'm not sure why this idea is hot, but my pussy is already getting ideas and we haven't even gotten to the good part yet.

I set my heels by the entrance. The hardwood is cool under my bare feet. I smooth my skirt, lower myself to my knees, and—

Ow.

The floor is harder than expected. My kneecaps lodge an immediate protest. I shift, trying to find a position that doesn't feel like medieval torture.

What if I'm doing this wrong? Is there's a technique to kneeling that submissives learn and nobody told me? What if he's watching on some hidden camera, grading my form? *C-minus, Elise, your posture is tragic.*

Stop.

I fold my hands in my lap. Straighten my spine. Breathe.

Minutes pass. Five. Maybe ten. My knees ache worse and my brain keeps trying to spiral—Lydia's smile, the way she said *invested*, the calculating look in her eyes—but then something strange happens.

The spiraling slows.

The quiet settles. Not the anxious silence of waiting to be judged. Something deeper. Something that feels almost like...peace.

By the time I hear his footsteps approaching, I'm feeling almost Zen. My shoulders have dropped. The anxiety I carried from catastrophizing Lydia's pointed comments is gone.

Sebastian appears in front of me, and strokes my hair.

"Good girl."

My entire body lights up, and my clit pulses like it has opinions about floor-kneeling. Apparently it's a fan.

"Stand."

I rise on unsteady legs. He catches my elbow, making sure I don't fall.

"The waiting didn't make me anxious." I lean into his chest and breathe his scent deeply. He always smells so good. "It calmed me."

"It transitioned you." He guides me toward the kitchen. "The ritual tells your brain to let go of everything outside and exist only here, with me."

He's right. Nothing matters but us in our little bubble.

Tonight, to my surprise, there's no sex. He makes dinner while I sit at the counter, and we talk about nothing important. A restaurant we both want to try. A client meeting that almost went sideways.

I watch his hands as he cooks, and think about the pleasure those hands have given me.

Focus, Elise.

After dinner, he settles in a plush chair by the window with a stack of reports. "Come here."

I kneel beside him. Not in front. Beside. My head rests against his thigh. His hand finds my hair and strokes in soothing patterns while he reads.

The city lights glitter beyond the glass. My eyes grow heavy as a languid fuzziness steals over me.

This is the strangest thing I've ever done with a man.

Not the kneeling. Not the waiting. This—this quiet intimacy. Being near him without needing to be anything other than what I am.

I fall asleep with my cheek on his thigh and his fingers tangled in my hair.

Friday at lunchtime, Tessa catches me on the way to the break room.

"Come with me." She's already moving before I can answer. "I need coffee that doesn't taste like motor oil, and you look like you need to talk."

We end up at a café two blocks from the office. We order, and she steers me to a secluded table.

"Spill." She sets down her cup. "What's eating you?"

"Lydia." The name tastes sour. "I don't like that she's implying that Sebastian and I..."

"That you're fucking your way to success?" Tessa's blunt, but her eyes are kind. "That woman is a viper."

"He defended me publicly. Which means she has more ammunition now." I wrap my hands around my cup, needing the warmth. "Does she know about us?"

"She suspects."

My stomach clenches. "We've been careful."

"You've been discreet. There's a difference." Tessa holds up a hand. "I'm not saying she has proof, but she seems to be looking for it."

Great. This is exactly what I needed today—confirmation that the woman who hates me is actively hunting for evidence that I'm banging the boss.

Which I am. Enthusiastically. But that's beside the point.

"What do I do?"

"Your job. Brilliantly. Give her nothing to use." Tessa's expression softens. "And lean on the people who have your back. You're not alone in this. Sebastian's team—we protect our own."

Our own.

The words land somewhere deeper than I expected, somewhere that's been empty for a long time.

"Why are you helping me?" The question slips out before I can stop it. "You barely know me."

"I told you someone helped me once." Tessa meets my eyes. "When I was new to Seth, new to the lifestyle, convinced I was broken for wanting what I wanted. A woman I barely knew sat me down and told me I wasn't and that I deserved to be loved exactly as I am." She smiles warmly. "She's the reason I'm still with Seth."

My throat tightens. "Thank you."

She raises her cup. "To the family you choose."

I clink my cup against hers.

The coffee is too sweet. But I drink it anyway, and for the first time in a very long time, I don't feel like I'm doing this alone.

CHAPTER 9

The afternoon crawls.

Lydia's been circling the office, and it's making me uncomfortable. Three times now, she's paused behind my chair, long enough to read my screen, long enough to make my shoulders knot. Each time, she hums a little like she's cataloging evidence.

My jaw aches from clenching. I keep imagining her CCing senior leadership on some email I haven't seen yet. Subject line: Concerns About Junior Staff. Or maybe she really is building a case. Maybe she's been building it since I took the promotion and had the audacity to be competent at things she expected me to fail at.

Half of me wants to spin around and ask what the fuck her problem is. The other half knows that's exactly what she wants. I recognize a trap when I see one, it's something I dealt with regularly during my years in the foster system. *Keep your head down. Don't make waves. Don't give them a reason.*

So I stare at my spreadsheet until the numbers blur.

When Sebastian's text arrives at four, I nearly knock my water bottle over lunging for my phone.

Sebastian: After work. My place.

Four words. My pussy reads them like a love letter. She's already voted yes, even though my brain is stuck on how brusque the words are. Between Lydia and now this text, I start spiraling.

This is where he tells me it's over. That this was a mistake. That a man like him can't actually be seen with someone like me, not in any way that matters.

I stare at the text for a full thirty seconds, waiting for the follow-up. The "we need to talk" that will shatter everything.

Nothing comes.

So either he's ending it, or he's not. Very helpful, brain. Thank you for that analysis.

I knock on his door at six-fifteen, still in my work clothes, still half-convinced I'm about to get a breakup speech.

He opens the door holding a flogger.

Okay. Probably not a breakup, then. Unless this is the kinkiest rejection in human history, which, honestly? Would be on brand for my life.

The flogger has dozens of soft leather strips hanging from a braided handle that sway when Sebastian shifts his grip. My pulse kicks against my throat, and my mouth is bone dry.

I said I wanted to try a flogger, and I meant it. But now that this thing is right in front of me, my brain is doing that helpful thing where it generates seventeen worst-case scenarios in three seconds flat. What if it hurts more than I think? What if I panic? What if I cry and he realizes I'm too broken for this and decides he'd rather fuck someone who doesn't come with emotional baggage the size of a small country?

"Touch it."

He holds it out like he's offering me a gift. My fingers slide through the suede falls. They're softer than I expected. Heavy, though. The bundle of leather cascades through my palm, and my clit pulses, fully on board with a flogging.

"This isn't punishment." His voice is steady. Patient. "This is sensation. The impact is different from my hand. More diffuse. Warmer." He drags the leather across my palm, and a shiver chases down my spine. "A good flogger disperses the force across your skin. Works into the muscle. It can be almost meditative once you surrender to the rhythm."

"Meditative." My laugh comes out breathy. "Is that what we're calling getting hit with a bunch of leather strips? Very Zen."

His mouth curves. That almost-smile that makes me want to earn the full thing. "You'll see. Want a demonstration?"

My breath catches, and I nod. He lifts the flogger, brings it down against my clothed thigh in a demonstration stroke.

The impact thuds through my muscle. No sting. Weight and warmth blooming outward.

"Oh."

That one syllable comes out way too pornographic. Great. Very dignified.

"This one isn't designed for pain. If you like it, we can work up to others over time." His thumb traces the handle. "Still green?"

I answer before I can second-guess myself. "Yes, I want to try."

His pupils dilate until the gray is nearly gone. That look. The one that makes me feel like prey. The one that makes me want to be caught.

"Strip. Then face the wall, hands braced at shoulder height."

My fingers tremble on the buttons of my blouse. The anticipation is so sharp it borders on pain. Each layer I remove is another wall coming down. Blouse first, folded on the couch because even now I want to be good for him. Bra next, nipples tightening immediately in the cool air. My skirt pools at my feet, and my panties are soaked through and cling to me when I peel them away.

Once I'm naked, I move to the wall he indicated. Behind me, the soft rustle of fabric as he rolls up his sleeves.

Cool plaster meets my palms as goosebumps rise across my skin. Every nerve ending is awake and waiting.

"Feet apart."

My stance spreads. I'm exposed and vulnerable with my ass and pussy on display for him. Arousal slicks down the inside of my thigh. I'm literally dripping for a man who's about to flog me. And the fucked up part is how right it feels.

My clit pulses with each heartbeat. My ass is already tingling in anticipation even though my brain keeps insisting this is supposed to be scary, right? Isn't this the part where I'm supposed to be nervous?

Tessa said this was okay. Tessa said there was nothing wrong with wanting this. I'm choosing to believe her, even though every foster home, every judgmental look, every time I was too much or too weird or too desperate is screaming that I should feel ashamed for wanting to submit like this.

Especially to the man who is my boss.

His hands land on my shoulders first. Warm. Grounding. He traces down my spine, counting each vertebra with his fingertips. Over my ribs. Across the swell of my hips. Down to my thighs and up again.

"I'm going to start with my hands to warm you up. You don't have to count tonight. Focus on breathing and how your body responds."

"Okay." My voice sounds far away, underwater.

The first smack lands on my right cheek. Light. Testing. Heat spreads like a starburst, and my breath stutters.

"Perfect. Breathe through it."

He builds a rhythm. Alternating sides. Never the same spot twice in a row. Each strike sends heat radiating outward, warming me from the outside in. My skin glows until every nerve buzzes and my pussy throbs with neglected need.

By the time he pauses, I'm already floating, half-gone to that quiet place he's shown me. The place where my thoughts stop spiraling and my body becomes pure sensation.

"Color."

"Green." The word comes out slow and dreamy.

"Now for the flogger."

The first stroke whispers across my shoulders.

A gasp escapes, but not from pain. From the weight of it, the way the leather spreads across my skin and leaves warmth in its wake. He was right; it's different. His hand is sharp and direct. This is broader. Deeper. The impact resonates into my muscles, loosening tension I didn't know I was carrying.

The second stroke is harder. Still on my shoulders, building heat.

A moan tears free. I can't help it. Don't want to help it.

"That's the sound I want." His voice wraps around me.

He finds a rhythm. Shoulders. The curve of my ass. Thighs. Each stroke lands with thudding warmth, building layer upon layer until my skin hums. The falls kiss and sting and soothe all at once. My thoughts scatter, and I don't try to catch them.

"Stay with me." His voice anchors me. "Breathe."

Time dissolves. It could be minutes, could be hours. There is only sensation. Only the weight of leather and the heat blooming across my skin. Only Sebastian's voice checking in, pulling me back when I drift too far.

"Still with me?"

"Mmmm." Words are hard. Everything is soft and far away.

"Color, Elise. I need words."

"Green." It takes effort to form the syllable. "Don't stop. Please don't stop."

The strokes move lower to my thighs again. The crease where my ass meets my legs. The soft, fleshy parts of my body that make me jolt and whimper.

I'm floating. Higher than before. The mental chatter that never stops, the constant narration of inadequacy and fear, is totally silent.

And in that silence, I finally understand.

This. This is why I crave it. Not the pain. Not even the pleasure.

The silence.

The permission to stop holding myself together. To stop being independent and pretending I'm fine and don't need anyone in a world that never bothered to catch me when I fell.

To let go. And be held.

Tears spill down my cheeks in release. Twenty-six years of keeping every crack plastered over and painted. From a childhood where crying meant weakness and weakness meant they'd send you to another home. Where being too much or too little or too anything at all was a risk you couldn't afford.

I'm sobbing now. Full body shaking. And the relief is so overwhelming I can barely breathe.

Sebastian stops immediately. The flogger drops. His hands cup my shoulders, and he turns me, pulling me against his chest.

"Hey. Hey." His voice is urgent. "Talk to me. What do you need?"

"Good tears." The words barely form between sobs. "I promise. These are good tears."

I'm getting snot on his shirt. His very expensive shirt. This is definitely what he signed up for when he decided to dom the emotionally stunted foster kid. Lucky him.

He exhales and holds me more tightly. Strokes my hair and doesn't rush me to explain or pull myself together. His solid warmth is steady.

We stand there long enough for my sobs to quiet. Long enough for my shaking to still. When I finally surface, he doesn't let go.

"Sorry about your shirt," I mumble into his chest. "I can pay for dry cleaning. Or a replacement. Or a new identity so you never have to see me ugly-cry again."

"Elise." His voice is rough. "Stop."

"Okay." I sniffle.

He lifts me, carries me to the bedroom, and settles me against the pillows on the bed. I let him, because my legs have apparently retired from active duty.

He disappears briefly. Returns with lotion that smells like lavender and a glass of water.

"Drink."

I obey. The cold helps.

"Now lie on your stomach."

I'm boneless and wrung out as I roll over. He spreads cool lotion across my heated skin, working it into the muscles where the flogger kissed. His touch is gentle, and he's treating every inch of reddened skin like it's precious.

I can't hold in the groan of relief.

"Do you want to talk about it?" His voice is quiet. No pressure.

"I figured it out." My words are muffled by the pillow. "Why I need this."

His hands pause for a moment before resuming their soothing path. "Tell me."

"I spent my whole childhood being quiet and easy so no one would have a reason to send me away." It's hard to talk about, but I want to tell him. "I got really good at holding everything together because if I fell apart, there was no one who cared."

His exhale is rough. His hands are gentle on my tender skin.

"Every foster home, every school, every job. I learned to be whoever they needed me to be." My throat tightens. "I'm so tired of holding myself so carefully that I never break."

"Elise." His voice cracks on my name.

"And then you." I turn my head to look at him. His expression is stripped of all its careful control. "You asked me to break on purpose. You held me while I did it. You're still holding me."

He pulls me up, turns me, cradles me against his chest. His arms wrap around me like he's afraid I'll disappear. "You can break with me. I'll always be here."

Half of me believes him. The other half is waiting for the fine print that says this offer expires when he realizes how much work I am.

But I'm tired of listening to that half.

"I believe you." The words come out broken. "I actually believe you."

He holds me more tightly and presses his lips to my hair. We stay like that until my breathing steadies and the tears dry on my cheeks.

Later, we're still in bed.

His hand traces lazy circles on my stomach. The touch is soft after the earlier intensity. Contemplative. My skin still hums from the flogger, but it's a relaxing warmth.

"I've been thinking about something." His voice is quiet. Almost careful.

"About what?"

His palm presses flat against my belly and holds there. "About building something permanent with you."

Fuck.

The image blooms in my mind before I can stop it. Me, round with his child. Him watching with that possessive hunger in his eyes while my belly grows.

My body buzzes. Not because I should want this, or because it's romantic. Because I want to be full of him. I want him to knock me up. I want to be his in every possible way, including the biological ones.

"That's..." I don't know how to finish.

"Too much?" He pulls his hand away. "I shouldn't have—"

"No." I grab his wrist, press his palm back to my stomach. "Not too much. I like the thought."

Understatement of the century. My ovaries are ready to do a hula dance and invite everyone to the luau.

His whole body goes still. "You do?"

"I never let myself want anything permanent." My hand covers his on my belly. "But with you, I'm starting to imagine things I never let myself want before."

Things like waking up next to him every morning. Things like tiny clothes and midnight feedings and a home that actually feels like home.

He pulls me closer and presses his forehead to mine.

"Not yet." His voice is rough. "But if this continues, someday."

"Someday." I breathe the word like a promise.

"When you know in your bones that this is permanent." He kisses me softly. "Then I'm going to give you everything. A ring. A family. A future where you never have to wonder if you belong."

Tears prick my eyes again. "I want all of it."

"Then trust me." He rolls me beneath him, settles between my thighs. "Trust that this is real."

"I'm trying."

"I know." He kisses my nose. "We have time."

When he puts on a condom and slides into me, his eyes stay on mine as he thrusts into me slowly. The pleasure builds in waves, cresting and ebbing, and when I finally shatter, it's with his name on my lips and his hand pressed flat against my belly.

I wake in the middle of the night with his arms around me. The room is dark. His breathing is steady. But his grip hasn't loosened, even in sleep.

Twenty-six years of being forgettable. Of slipping through cracks. Of being easy to leave.

And this man holds me like he's terrified to let go.

This seems crazy fast. A few weeks ago, I was eating a birthday cupcake alone, and now I'm naked in my boss's bed, thinking about having his babies. If someone told me this was my future, I would have laughed until I cried.

But it feels right. It feels like *finally*.

His hand is still on my stomach. I think about having his cum inside me. Actual breeding. The thought thrills me, and I press my thighs together.

Tomorrow I'm calling my doctor to get on the pill. I might not be ready to get pregnant yet, but I want his cum inside me.

Chapter 10

The rules seemed simple when we made them.

Text Sebastian when I leave work. Don't skip meals. Tell him when I'm spiraling instead of withdrawing. Three guidelines that we negotiated together and are written in my phone's notes app like a contract I signed with my entire stupid heart.

They're not restrictions. They're safety nets. A way for him to take care of me when I forget to take care of myself.

Which, as it turns out, is basically my entire personality. Someone should put that on my tombstone. "Here lies Elise Hart. She forgot to eat lunch and died. Again."

Growing up, I could skip dinner for a week, and no one would notice. I could stay out until midnight at twelve years old because no one was checking. If I failed a class or aced one, I'd receive the same blank response from whatever adult was supposed to be paying attention. I know there are plenty of good foster parents, but the ones I was placed with had too many kids. My teachers had too many students. Everyone had better things to do than keep track of one quiet girl who never caused problems.

I learned early that if I wanted boundaries, I'd have to build them myself. If I wanted accountability, I'd have to be my own enforcer. And I was terrible at it. Still am. If left to my own devices, I'll work until I collapse, skip meals until I'm shaking, and convince myself that survival mode is just a normal Tuesday.

Sebastian's rules aren't to control me. They're the opposite of everything I've ever known. For the first time in my life, someone's invested enough to make sure I'm taking care of myself.

But this week, work has been a nightmare.

Lydia Kessler has made it her personal mission to question every decision I make. She CCs half the company on passive-aggressive corrections, schedules meetings that conflict with my deadlines, and smiles at me in the hallway like we're sorority sisters who share lipstick.

Monday, she suggested my projections were "optimistic" in front of the entire team. Her smile never wavered. Neither did my desire to throw my laptop at her perfectly styled head. Tuesday, she requested I redo the vendor analysis with "more conservative assumptions." By Wednesday, I was second-guessing numbers I'd triple-checked and fantasizing about her falling into a very deep hole.

I can picture her face right now. That perfectly lipsticked smile while she tells the board I'm incompetent. I can see her building a case, brick by brick, an evidence folder growing fatter by the day. *See? She never belonged here. She got lucky. She sucked the boss's dick for her promotion, and now we have proof.*

My shoulders have taken up permanent residence somewhere near my earlobes. The stress coils tighter with each passing hour, and my stomach hasn't unknotted since Monday morning.

I did manage one thing for myself this week: I slipped out during lunch on Monday to the clinic and got on the pill. The small packet sits in my purse, three days of pills already gone.

The thought of ditching the condoms, of having nothing between us—my pussy perks up like she heard her name called. Down, girl. We're spiraling about work right now, not about Sebastian's cock filling me up with cum while he tells me he's going to get me pregnant. We have priorities here.

I've been waiting to tell Sebastian. But with Lydia breathing down my neck and my stress levels through the roof, the timing hasn't felt right to bring up the whole "I'm ready for you to fuck me raw and come inside me" conversation. Very romantic. Definitely the kind of pillow talk that screams "I'm a well-adjusted adult."

And somewhere in the chaos, I forget the rules.

By Thursday night, I'm barely functional.

My computer screen blurs at the edges. I've read the same paragraph six times and absorbed exactly none of it. Blinking doesn't help. Rubbing my eyes doesn't help. My brain has left the building and forgotten to take my body with it.

I check the time.

10:14 PM.

The office is empty. When did everyone leave? The fluorescent lights hum overhead, and it's making my budding headache worse. My coffee went cold hours ago. A granola bar wrapper on my desk mocks me.

C-minus, Elise. D for nutrition. F for basic self-preservation.

My hand reaches for my phone to check tomorrow's calendar. That's when I see the notifications. Three texts from Sebastian. Sent hours ago.

6:47 PM: Leaving soon?

8:22 PM: Elise. Check in.

9:58 PM: I'm coming to find you.

Ice floods my veins.

Four hours of radio silence when I promised I'd check in. And dinner—trying to remember the last thing I ate. The granola bar at eleven this morning. Maybe some crackers from the break room around two. Maybe. The memory is fuzzy, which probably means it didn't happen.

Great. Perfect. I've managed to worry the one person who actually gives a shit about me. Achievement unlocked: Professional and Personal Disappointment.

This is the part where Sebastian realizes I'm too much work. Too broken. Too incapable of doing one simple thing like texting him when I leave my desk. This is the part where he looks at me with those gray eyes and says this was fun but he needs someone less exhausting. Someone who can remember to eat lunch without a reminder. Someone who doesn't spiral at the first sign of stress like a defective toy.

My fingers shake as I type.

Elise: I'm so sorry. Lost track of time. I'm fine. Still at the office.

His response comes in seconds.

Sebastian: Come to my office. Now.

What is he doing here at the office this late? My pulse trips as dread tangles with anticipation in a combination my body has no business feeling.

I broke the rules.

We talked about consequences if I broke them, and punishment was part of the negotiation. Not because he wants to hurt me. Because the structure matters and the boundaries keep me safe and help him take care of his submissive.

And because—this is the part I've never admitted out loud—I want someone to hold me accountable and to notice if I disappear. I enjoy having Sebastian text me and ask me where I'm at if I'm running late, or check in to make sure I've eaten. Having someone who worries about you is a kind of care I've never known.

When Sebastian makes rules, he's saying I matter to him. If he follows through with the consequences, he's proving that someone is finally paying attention.

My hands tremble as I gather my things. The building is quiet at this hour, and my heels echo in the empty hallway. A security guard nods as I pass, but otherwise, I'm alone with my racing thoughts.

He's going to end this. He's going to look at me with disappointment in those gray eyes and say—

Stop. Focus, Elise.

Half of me wants to run to his office and apologize until my throat is raw. The other half wants to run in the opposite direction and never face the look on his face when he realizes how fundamentally broken I am.

The elevator ride seems shorter than usual. Sebastian's door is open and light spills into the corridor.

"Sebastian?"

He's standing by the window, jacket off, sleeves rolled to his elbows. His silhouette is sharp against the city lights. When he turns, his expression is carefully blank.

"Come in. Close the door."

His voice is level. Controlled. Somehow that's worse than if he were shouting.

I shut the door behind me.

"Explain." He stares at me, and I can't tell how angry he is.

"I lost track of time." The excuse sounds pathetic even to me. "Lydia's been...the Catalyst project needed revisions...I was trying to—"

"Did any of that prevent you from taking thirty seconds to text me?"

My throat tightens. "No."

"Did you eat dinner?"

Can't meet his eyes. "I meant to."

"That's not what I asked." He moves closer. "Look at me, Elise."

Forcing my gaze up takes effort. His jaw is tight. His eyes are hard. But underneath, I can see the worry.

He was scared.

"The rules exist because I care about you." His voice is low. Intense. "When you don't follow them, you're telling me your well-being doesn't matter. That you don't matter." He cups my jaw, tilting my face up. "That's unacceptable."

Tears prick at my eyes. "I didn't think. I'm sorry."

"I know you are." His thumb brushes my cheek. "You're still getting punished."

The words settle in my chest. Heavy. Right.

"Yes, Sir."

The other times he's spanked me, there was playfulness. Build-up and teasing and orgasms that shattered me apart. This is discipline, not play.

The distinction clicks as I stand before him. This won't end with an orgasm.

Shame weighs me down, but relief lives right beside it. When this is done, the guilt won't be mine to carry anymore. He's taking it from me.

He guides me to his desk. "Tell me which rules you broke." His voice is steady, but there's a strained tightness underneath.

My cheeks burn. "I didn't text you to tell you I was staying late at work. I skipped dinner. I withdrew instead of telling you I was struggling."

"All three." He exhales slowly. "In one night."

Three promises I made and broke. Hearing them listed out loud makes the weight of it land harder.

"Lift your skirt. Bend over."

My hands obey before my brain can catch up. The cool air hits my thighs as I fold forward, my palms pressing flat against the wood. My panties are thin. Barely a barrier.

"Fifteen." His hand rests on the small of my spine. Grounding. "You'll count. If you lose count, we start over."

"Yes, Sir."

Behind me, I hear him draw a breath. When his palm finally lifts from my spine, I catch the slight tremor in his fingers.

This costs him too.

Maybe not in the same way it costs me, but the toll is real.

His jaw is set when I glance over my shoulder. The muscle there ticks with tension. He meets my eyes for one moment, and I see it: the iron control it takes to be what I need right now.

There's no warm-up this time. The first strike lands hard across my right cheek, and I gasp at the impact.

"One."

The second falls on the left. Harder than expected. Heat flares through my skin.

"Two."

He finds a steady rhythm. Not brutal, but firm.

"Three. Four."

By five, my eyes are stinging. Not from the pain—the pain is bearable, familiar—but from the knowledge I was careless with myself.

"Five." The word splinters in my mouth.

The tears start falling.

"Six. Seven. Eight."

Each count comes out rougher than the last, and I'm crying. I treated myself like garbage. Skipped meals because who cares, right? Worked until I made myself sick because my health doesn't matter. Struggled alone because I'm not used to having anyone who actually gives a shit.

"Nine. Ten."

A sob tears out of me. This isn't the hazy, floaty feeling when he spanks me for fun. This goes straight to the core. All the guilt I've been hauling around, for tonight and for every time I've let myself down, spills out like poison draining from an old wound.

All these years of punishing myself for existing because no one else thought I was worth the effort.

"Eleven. Twelve. Thirteen."

I'm shaking, clinging to the desk while tears stream down my face. I don't want them to stop. For the first time, I'm grieving all the ways I've treated myself like I was worthless.

"Fourteen."

The final strike lands, and I sob the last number.

"Fifteen."

He immediately gathers me up and pulls me from the desk, cradling me against his chest as I fall apart.

"It's over." His voice is rough. "It's done now. Forgiven."

Forgiven.

The word breaks me open.

The guilt that's lived in my chest for as long as I can remember has gone quiet. That constant hum of not being enough, not trying hard enough, not mattering enough. I don't have to punish myself or spiral or convince myself I'm terrible. The slate is clean.

And now I'm being held. I didn't expect the release.

I'm crying into his chest and probably wrecking his shirt, but he's not letting go. He just holds me more tightly and murmurs, "You're okay. I promise you're okay," into my hair. Right now, his arms feel like the only real thing in the world.

He carries me to the couch and sits, settling me in his lap. A blanket gets tucked around my shoulders. I don't know where it came from, and I don't care. He just holds me while the sobs slow to hiccups and then stop altogether.

"Talk to me." He strokes my back in slow, steady passes. "How do you feel?"

"Lighter." The word surprises me, but it's true. "Also disgusting. I'm pretty sure I got snot on your shirt. And your desk. I should come with a warning label. *Caution: May leak at high emotional altitudes.*"

His chest vibrates with a quiet laugh. "All of that can be cleaned."

"I'm sorry—"

"Stop." His arms tighten. "The slate is clean, Elise. Completely clean. Do you understand?"

I nod against his chest. The part of me that was braced for disappointment finally lets go.

"I need to hear you say it." His voice is gentle but firm.

"The slate is clean." My voice wobbles but holds. "I'm forgiven."

"Good girl." He kisses my hair. "That's exactly right."

We snuggle together on the couch. After a few minutes, he disappears and comes back with a container of pasta from the executive fridge, part of the stash he keeps for working late. He holds the fork out while I'm still curled against him, too wrung out to do anything but open my mouth.

"Eat." The command is soft. "All of it."

I obey. Each bite settles the emptiness in my stomach. Between bites, he makes me drink an entire bottle of water.

When the container is empty, he sets it aside and pulls me into his lap. His chin rests on top of my head. His chest rises and falls in a rhythm I've grown to know.

"I was worried." There's a tremor in his voice I've never heard before. "When you didn't answer, I thought..." He doesn't finish. Just swallows and holds me more tightly.

When I lift my head to look at him, his expression is completely unguarded. The mask he usually wears is gone.

"You thought I left."

His jaw tightens. "I thought you were pulling away. That I'd pushed too hard."

Sebastian Ashford, who controls everything, was afraid. Afraid I'd disappeared. Afraid he'd lost me.

"I called the security desk first," he admits quietly. "They said you were still here."

The words hit me. He was that scared. I did that to him.

"I'm not leaving." Pressure builds behind my eyes. "I was...forgetting I matter."

"You matter." The words are a growl. "Don't forget again."

"I won't." And this time, I mean it.

He presses his lips to my forehead for a long moment. When he pulls away, his eyes are softer.

"Next time you're overwhelmed, you tell me. Even if you think it's stupid. That's what the rules are for." He pauses. "That's what I'm for."

A nod against his chest. "I will."

We sit like that for a while. His heartbeat is steady under my ear. My ass throbs from the discipline, but the pain is distant. All that remains is peace.

"Lydia," I say finally. "She's been making everything harder. Questioning my work. Undermining me in meetings. I didn't want to tell you because..."

"Because you thought you had to handle it yourself."

I wince. "Yes."

"I'll deal with Lydia." His voice hardens. "But right now, I want you to understand: even when work is hard, even when someone is making your life difficult, you don't punish yourself by not eating." He tilts my chin up. "I want to know when you're struggling."

My eyes sting again. "I'm not used to people wanting to be let in."

"Get used to it." He kisses me softly. "I'm not going anywhere."

Eventually, we leave. Sebastian keeps his hand on the small of my spine as we walk to the elevator. The security guard raises an eyebrow when we pass, but I don't care. Let him think what he wants. I know what this is.

In the parking garage, Sebastian opens the passenger door of his car. I slide in, my ass sore in a way that will remind me of this night tomorrow. He rounds to the driver's side and settles behind the wheel but doesn't start the engine.

The silence stretches. Not uncomfortable, but weighted. Like he's deciding whether to say what comes next.

"I have a playroom I haven't shown you yet." His voice is quiet. "When you're ready."

My breath catches.

A playroom. That came up in my research. Dedicated space, actual equipment, not just making do in his bedroom or office. The fact that he's telling me now, after everything tonight, means he thinks I can handle whatever he has in there. But it's more than that. He's letting me further into his world, and that realization sends warmth spreading through me.

"I'm ready."

His eyes hold mine in the dim light of the garage. "Are you?"

Half of me is screaming *yes, finally, more.* The other half is doing anxious math about how many different ways I could embarrass myself in a room full of equipment I've only seen on the internet.

But tonight has shown me that I'm ready for everything he has to give.

"Yes." The word comes out steady. "I'm ready."

"Then we'll play this weekend."

He starts the car and takes my hand across the console. He holds my hand most of the drive home—his home. We didn't talk about it, but we both know I'm spending the night with him.

Tonight, the silence in my head feels different. Not empty. Warm. Like I've found where I'm supposed to be.

CHAPTER 11

I spent last night doing more research, this time on BDSM playrooms and dungeons. It was three hours of bondage furniture websites, online forums, and one instructional video I closed after forty-five seconds because my face was so hot I thought I might combust.

Not that my brain could stick to one obsession at a time. Somewhere between leather restraint systems and impact play tutorials, work crept back in.

The Nelson acquisition is the deal everyone's watching. Forty-two million dollars, a manufacturing company with three hundred employees, and a founder who's turned down two buyers already because she didn't trust their plans for her people. Sebastian wants me to build the integration strategy—org restructuring, systems migration, the whole transition timeline. If I nail this, I prove I earned my promotion. If I don't, Lydia's whisper campaign writes itself.

But I'm not thinking about Nelson or Lydia or org charts right now. I'm thinking about the man waiting for me and whatever he has planned.

As soon as I get to his condo, I take my heels off and kneel in the entryway until Sebastian comes for me. Now he's following me down the hallway toward a door I've always assumed was a spare room.

Half of me is screaming *turn around, this is too much, you're not actually the kind of woman who gets strapped to medieval torture equipment*. The other half—my pussy—is already wet. That's the half that's controlling my legs. No matter how scary this is, I want it and I trust him.

I breathe deeply as we walk. I try thinking about safety protocols or whatever responsible BDSM practitioners should be thinking about. But his thumb is tracing small circles against my spine, and all I can think about is how I want that thumb about six inches lower and a lot less gentle.

Focus, Elise.

We haven't spoken since I got here. He told me tonight would be different, and the silence is working me up more than all my research. My nipples are tight, and my pulse kicks hard under my ribs. We haven't even gotten to the door yet, and my panties are already soaked.

He stops and pulls a key from his pocket. "Elise." The hoarseness in his voice is so damn sexy and makes my brain go offline. "Look at me."

I hold his gaze. If he's searching for doubt, he's not going to find any. What he'll see is a woman who researched spanking benches like she was shopping for a new car and is currently buzzing with equal parts nerves and desire.

"What happens in this room, there's no judgment or shame. If you want to stop at any point, say the word, and we walk out. Understood?"

"Yes, Sir."

"What's your color right now?"

"Very green." It's a miracle that my voice isn't shaking.

The corner of his mouth curves before he unlocks the door and steps aside. "Ladies first."

I'm practically buzzing from curiosity, but the room is nothing like I expected. It's not some red-lit cliché dungeon. There are three walls in deep charcoal, and one in exposed brick. The dark laminate floor has a thick gray rug. The lighting is a soft warmth without harsh shadows. It smells like leather and lemon cleaner.

Against one wall is a daybed piled with soft blankets that looks perfect for fucking, but my gaze lands on the St. Andrew's Cross mounted against the far wall. I only know what it is from my research. It's ebony-stained oak with leather padding for the wrists and ankles. The steel hardware catches the light. My clit throbs and my brain short-circuits somewhere between run and climb on immediately.

"Take your time," Sebastian says from behind me. "Examine whatever you want and ask me anything."

The St. Andrew's Cross dominates the space, and I can't stop staring at it.

"That's the centerpiece." His voice is warm at my ear. "I had it custom built."

I make myself walk further into the room. If I keep staring at that cross, I'm going to forget how to breathe. There's a black leather spanking bench to my left, and I run my fingers over the leather.

"How does this one work?" I know the general idea, but I need a moment to compose myself.

"You'd kneel here." He taps the padded shelf. "Chest goes on this section, arms through here." His hand traces the path my body would take. "There are restraints, and it positions you perfectly for impact, penetration, or both."

Both. My entire body zings at the thought of being strapped in while he fucks me. I'm pretty sure these panties are ruined, but that's a problem for future Elise.

A glass-door cabinet catches my attention next. Floggers hang in a neat row, arranged by weight, and various-sized paddles line the shelf below. Coils of rope in burgundy, black, and purple are wound neatly.

I pause before opening the cabinet. "May I?"

"Explore everything."

The door opens silently, and I lift a flogger. It's heavier than I expected, and I brush the suede falls against my forearm, shivering at the softness.

He moves behind me, and his chest brushes against my back. "That's another sensation flogger like we used before."

I reach for a heavier leather one. My wrist dips under the weight.

"That one bites." His voice drops. "For when you're ready to feel the edge."

I hang it back carefully. Yeah, let's just put that right there. I'm not sure I want the bite. The drawer beneath holds smaller items. There's a wheel on a handle, like a pizza cutter, except the edge is covered in sharp metal points. Next to it are feathers, blindfolds, and nipple clamps ranging from gentle to intense. Everything is perfectly organized and pristine. I can tell they've never been used.

I reach for the sharp wheel in curiosity. "Can we try this one?"

When I peek over my shoulder at him, his gaze is heated.

"The Wartenberg wheel? Yes, we absolutely can."

Setting it back in its spot, I run my fingers over a feather tickler. "You built all of this for someone."

"For the right person. I've played with subs, but never here. I built this room for when I found someone I wanted to keep."

Wait. He hasn't brought anyone in here before? I look at him, and the expression on his face stops me cold. It's completely open and honest.

"I want to try out the cross." I blurt it out, needing to say something before this gets too intense.

He studies me for a long moment. "You're sure?"

"Yes." Because if I stay in this conversation another second, I'm going to ask questions I'm not sure I'm ready to hear the answers to.

He undresses me while I stand there forcing myself not to help. Each button gets his attention, and his fingers brush skin as my blouse falls away. He folds it neatly and sets it on a side table. My skirt, bra, and panties follow.

I stand before him, naked and trembling, while he's still fully dressed in jeans and a t-shirt. This isn't new since I'm naked while he stays clothed often. But the power imbalance still gets to me every time. The vulnerability lights me up from the inside out.

"Beautiful. Every inch of you." He breathes it like a prayer. "Now go to the cross, face it, and put your hands on the upper beams."

My legs carry me forward. The wood is cool against my palms while I wait.

"I'm going to restrain you now. Wrists first, then ankles. Don't forget to use your safewords if you need them." His hands settle on my hips. "If you can't speak, tap twice on the wood. I'll check in throughout. Understood?"

"Yes."

"Good girl."

The praise releases tension I didn't know I'd been carrying. He guides my right wrist into the upper cuff and adjusts the strap until it's snug but not cutting.

"Too tight?"

"No, it's good."

My left wrist follows before he kneels to spread my legs wider, securing each ankle with the same careful attention and testing the give.

When he's done, I'm splayed open against the cross with nothing to hide behind. This is the part where I'd assumed the reality of being restrained and completely vulnerable would trigger some survival instinct, but my pussy is dripping. I've never felt safer in my entire life.

The noise in my head goes quiet.

Not just quiet. Silent. My chest loosens. There's nothing but my heartbeat and the sound of his breathing behind me. I don't have to decide anything right now. I just have to be here and let him take care of what happens next.

His footsteps cross the room, and I hear the cabinet open before he returns. The feather touches me. It's a whisper down my spine, and I arch against the restraints. He traces my shoulder blade, the dip of my waist, the curve of my ass. It's maddening.

"Stay still," he murmurs. "You're mine to play with."

I try, but when the wheel replaces the feather, tiny sharp points rolling up my inner thigh, my hips jerk.

"You're sensitive here." There's a dark approval in his tone as he traces it higher.

Oh no.

Oh no no no.

That's heading in a direction I didn't expect, and I did NOT mentally prepare for pointy wheel meets sensitive bits.

Do people put that thing on their pussy? Is that a thing? That's definitely a thing, isn't it? I should have researched this. Why didn't I? Jesus, I need to safeword. Any second now. Right after I find out if this is going to hurt or make me come. It could go either way.

He stops before it touches anything too sensitive. I shiver and moan, half in disappointment. Fuck, that's messed up.

"Sebastian—"

"Patience."

I don't have patience. I have a throbbing clit and zero chill, but I want to please him.

The feather sweeps my shoulders, and then the wheel traces my ribs, sharp then soft, soft then sharp, in no pattern, until I'm trembling. Every nerve is screaming, and I can't tell pleasure from torment.

"Please, please, please."

"Please what?"

"More. I need—" I don't really know what I'm asking for. "I need more."

"Good girl."

His hand trails down my back, and he stops at the base. "I want to hear you throughout. Moans, words, screams. Whatever you need. If you go quiet, I'll check in."

"Yes, Sir."

"That's my girl."

The first spank makes me gasp in surprise. Warmth blooms across my skin. He does it again on the other cheek, building heat with each impact. My body rocks against the cross.

"Relax into it."

I breathe through each strike. The next one lands lower, catching the curve where my ass meets my thigh. I moan, and the sound echoes in the room.

"You're so gorgeous like this." His hand soothes where he spanked my ass. "Letting me use you however I want."

He spanks me until my skin is hot and tingling and I'm panting. My hips rock with each smack, desperate for friction.

"I'm going to use the flogger now. Be vocal and stay present."

The first stroke across my shoulders steals my breath. The strands spread the impact like a massage gone dark, warmth blooming in a wide band. I arch before I realize I'm moving.

He rotates between my shoulders, upper back, and the curve of my ass. Each stroke layers over the last until my skin is zinging and my thoughts slow.

The world narrows to the rhythm of leather meeting skin. I stop tracking time. Stop tracking anything except the sharp pleasure spreading through me. My arms pull against the cuffs, but they're keeping me exactly where I belong.

The flogger lands across my thighs, and I cry out from the intensity. The rush that follows wipes my mind clean. I'm floating as the heat spreads through me like liquid fire.

I've spent my life staying ready for the next crisis, but there's no crisis or threat here. There's only Sebastian. My breath deepens, and my muscles soften.

When the flogger stops, he runs his hands over my back, straight down between my legs. His fingers slip between my thighs, and I whimper in pleasure as he finger fucks me.

"Mmm. My little slut is soaking wet."

I try to rock against his hand. "Only for you."

He kisses my shoulder and growls. "Time to fuck my captive toy."

I hear him unzip his jeans and the crinkle of the condom package. His hard cock nudges my ass before sliding lower. He pushes the tip into my pussy, and then pulls out to slap his cock against my ass.

"Please," I moan, "I need you."

"Too bad you don't decide what you get tonight."

Fuuuuck. I pull against the restraints and writhe as he continues to tease me with just the tip. Each press against my pussy makes me think that this time he's finally going to slide all the way in. But the bastard just keeps rocking against me and driving me crazy.

The room spins, and I can hear myself begging. "Please, please, please, fuck me. Oh god, please."

He pulls all the way out again. "I'm not convinced you want this cock bad enough yet."

"Not convinced? Are you—?" He pushes the tip in, and I gasp. "Fuck, what do you need, a signed—?" Another shallow thrust that goes nowhere. "Oh god—a petition? I'll get signatures. I'll—" He rocks against me, teasing while my mind turns to mush. "Please—I'm begging here, and you're—" Another maddening press of just the tip. "You sadistic—please just fuck me."

Just when I'm about to promise my firstborn, he slides in slowly, inch by agonizing inch. I groan loudly and rock my ass backwards. When he bottoms out, I can't tell where he ends and I begin.

"So good." He grasps my hips, holding me still while he fucks me slowly. "I might just keep you like this all night. My cocksleeve."

Ohhhh god, I love it when he acts like he's going to use me whenever he wants. It drives me wild, and I whimper as he fucks me with long, deep strokes. I'm crying out every time he slides all the way in.

"Look at you. Bound and taking my cock like this is exactly where you belong."

"I do," I moan. "I belong to you. With you."

The words slip out before I can catch them, but they're true. I feel it in my bones, this strange, terrifying certainty that I've been searching for him without knowing it.

His rhythm falters a second before he fucks me harder. One hand fists in my hair, pulling my head back until my throat is exposed. His teeth graze my pulse.

"I want to keep you like this." His voice is ragged against my ear. "Tied up in my playroom. Wet and ready whenever I want."

"Yes. God, yes."

"I want to fill you so deep you feel me for days."

My pussy clenches around him.

"I want to breed you." The words rip out of him. "I want to watch your belly grow with my baby. I'll keep fucking you, filling you with my cum. Over and over."

"Yes, yes, yes." All I can do is chant. I want everything he's saying. He can tie me up, fuck me, breed me, keep me here and never let me go.

He slams into me, and suddenly an orgasm tears through me. I scream his name and come apart on his cock while he pounds into me, chasing his own release.

His hips stutter, slam deep, and he groans my name against my shoulder as he pulses inside me. We stay there, joined, shaking.

Time dissolves, and I don't know how long it is before he withdraws slowly. When I whimper, he kisses my shoulder. "I'm going to get you down now."

He kneels, and the cuff at my right ankle unbuckles with a soft click. His thumbs press into my calf, checking circulation. He rotates my foot gently and runs his thumb along the arch. My leg trembles.

"Mmm." My words are gone. Language is a distant concept. I know I used to know how to form sentences.

He releases my left ankle with the same care. "Good girl. Almost there."

He rises and takes the cuff off my right wrist. He catches my arm as it falls, massaging the joint, checking for marks as his thumb works into the muscle. He lifts my wrist to his mouth and kisses the faint pink indentation.

When the final restraint releases, I collapse against him. He catches me like I weigh nothing and lifts me against his chest. My limbs are liquid.

I press my face into his neck and breathe him in as he carries me over to the daybed. He settles me down on the soft blankets, and a second later, he's pressing a bottle of water against my lips.

"Drink."

I sip, and thoughts return through the haze.

He murmurs, "You did so well."

The praise wraps around me, warm and soft. I want to hold onto it. I want to live inside this feeling where everything is simple.

The arnica cream comes next. Warmed between his palms, then worked into my shoulders, my back, and the curves of my ass. He's tender as he cares for my marks.

Each stroke of his hands pulls me a little further out of the haze but doesn't break the spell. He's gentle with me, and I let myself be cared for without fighting it or wondering what I owe him in return.

When he's done, he stretches beside me and pulls me against his chest. His heartbeat slows beneath my ear, lulling me, and he strokes my hair.

He eventually asks, "How do you feel?"

My body is loose and humming. My mind is empty. "So good." I nestle deeper into his chest. "My head is never quiet except with you."

He kisses my head. "I want to tell you something." His voice rumbles through his chest. "And I need you to hear it without panicking."

I'm too relaxed to panic. "Mmm, okay."

"I really do want to give you a baby someday." His hand never stops stroking my hair. "And I want a future with you."

Oh.

My eyes sting. He's seen my ugly, scared parts and he still wants me anyway.

My voice is breathless and small when I respond. "I think I really want that too."

"So let's make a pact." He tilts my chin until I'm looking at him. The dominant is gone, and it's just Sebastian, the man, who is looking at me tenderly. "When you're ready, we start trying and build a family."

The tears spill before I can stop them. "Sebastian..."

"You don't have to answer now." His thumbs brush the wetness away. "I'm not asking for a commitment tonight. I'm asking you to consider it and let yourself want it without being afraid."

"But I'm terrified," I whisper. "I've wanted things before. And every time..."

"I'm not leaving." He responds to my unfinished thoughts. "And I'm telling you, Elise Hart, that as soon as you believe that, I'm going to breed you so hard, your head will spin."

I giggle as my tears dry. He's crazy in such a good way. I kiss his chest and let the happiness wash over me. This man is offering me everything I've never let myself want.

"Okay," I say finally. "When I'm ready, I'll let you know."

His mouth finds mine. "You won't regret it."

* * *

Later, after a shower and food, I'm curled into his bed while he's in the bathroom. I check my phone. Four missed texts.

Tessa: Team drinks Monday night.

Tessa: Daniel's buying.

Tessa: You're coming. No arguments.

I smile, and then see a text from an unknown number.

Unknown: Enjoy it while it lasts. Men like him always get bored.

My stomach drops. *Lydia.* It has to be. She's the only one who actively hates me. But how would she have my number?

My thumb hovers over the delete button. I could pretend I never saw the text. But I know the words are already branded into my brain where they'll live forever, rent-free, playing on loop at 3 a.m.

Men like him always get bored.

Of course they do. And why would he want me?

My chest is too tight. The room is too small. I should delete this and handle it alone the way I've handled everything my whole—

The bathroom door opens, and Sebastian walks in. He sees the look on my face, and he's at my side immediately, taking my hand in his.

"Whatever it is," he says, "we handle it together."

I show him the text, and my tender lover disappears as his jaw hardens and his eyes go cold.

"Lydia." His voice is barely contained rage. "She made a comment about you yesterday." He looks at me. "She's about to learn what happens when you threaten what's mine."

I almost tell him to let it go, that I can handle her. But then I remember his words in the playroom. He wants so much more when I'm ready. It's time to try something different with my life.

I lean into him and let him hold me. For the first time, I believe someone can protect me.

And I'm done pretending I don't want it.

CHAPTER 12

I wake up crying, and I don't know why. Tears slide down my face before I'm fully conscious. There's warm skin against my spine and the faint scent of familiar cedar body wash.

I'm safe in Sebastian's bed. Except my body missed that memo because the tears won't stop. My brain is screaming *what is happening* while my eyes continue leaking like a broken faucet I can't turn off.

"Hey." His voice is rough with sleep, and his arm tightens around my waist, pulling me closer. "Hey, baby. What's wrong?"

I cry harder, which makes me want to apologize for being insane. I want to explain that I'm not usually like this, except apparently I am, because here I am, sobbing into Sebastian's sheets at—what time is it?

"I don't—" My voice cracks. Yeah, that's attractive. "I don't know. I—"

Words won't form. There's only this rawness in my chest, like someone scraped out my insides and left the nerve endings exposed. My throat is thick with something I can't name. I'm a blotchy, hiccupping disaster, and he's getting a front row seat.

He hugs me close. "You might have subdrop."

He rolls me over to face him and cups my cheek. The gentleness makes me cry harder.

"Your body's processing what we did last night."

I sob. "We had an amazing night. Why do I feel like the world is ending?"

"This happens sometimes. It's normal." He kisses my forehead, lingering there like he has all the time in the world. Like a crying woman in his bed at dawn is perfectly acceptable. "After intense scenes, your body releases a lot of neurochemicals. When they drop, this can happen."

He wraps his arms around me like I'm worth protecting, even when I'm a mess. I keep waiting for him to sigh and give a polite suggestion that I pull myself together.

It doesn't come.

After a few minutes, I'm composed enough to ask, "What do I do?"

"You let me take care of you." His voice is firm and gentle at the same time, which doesn't seem possible, but somehow is. "I'll make you breakfast, and we'll stay in today. If you're still not better on Monday, we'll call in sick."

"You can't—" A hiccup breaks through the tears. "You have meetings. Important things."

"Nothing is more important than you."

He says it like it's obvious. Like rearranging a CEO's entire day because his submissive can't stop crying is perfectly reasonable.

I'm getting snot on his shoulder. This is definitely what he signed up for when he decided to take on a sub with attachment issues and zero experience being taken care of.

I press my face into his chest and let myself fall apart while he holds me and strokes my hair. He murmurs words I don't fully process but absorb anyway, somewhere deep in my bones.

"You're okay. I've got you. Let it out."

By the time the tears slow, I'm wrung out but somehow lighter. He kisses my forehead once more and slips out of bed.

My brain immediately starts its favorite game of 'What Does This Mean?'

He's still here. He watched me ugly-cry for—I squint at the clock on the nightstand—forty-five minutes, and he's still here. What does it mean that he's choosing this mess, choosing me, when he could have someone who doesn't fall apart after a night of—

The smell of eggs drifts in from the kitchen. A spatula clinks against a pan. He's making me breakfast.

I stop thinking and let myself breathe.

We spend Sunday morning on his couch, not doing anything productive, not even talking much. Just...existing together in matching sweatpants. He gave me a pair that I had to roll at the waist three times. I look ridiculous, but he keeps glancing at me, and his expression says I'm the sexiest thing he's ever seen.

My brain keeps insisting there must be a catch. I wish my brain would shut up.

He orders Thai food around noon. Pad see ew spring rolls and that coconut soup I mentioned loving once weeks ago, and apparently, he remembered. This man files away information about me like I'm a company he's planning to acquire.

Which, technically...

"How do you do that?" I ask, stirring my soup. "Remember the little things like the soup? The way I like my coffee. That I hate the sound of people chewing ice."

He shrugs, but there's something careful in the gesture. "I pay attention to the people who matter."

"Most people don't." I'm not fishing for reassurance. It's just a fact. Most people don't notice the small things, and if they do, they don't remember. "You'd think it would be standard operating procedure, but it's really not."

He's quiet for a moment, watching me with an expression I can't quite read.

"My mother taught me."

The words land strangely. He's never mentioned his parents. I assumed they were dead or estranged or one of those topics wrapped in caution tape. Sebastian doesn't volunteer personal information often.

"Your mother?"

"Eleanor." His voice softens on the name. "She adopted me when I was twelve."

The soup spoon freezes halfway to my mouth.

Adopted.

I set the spoon down, suddenly not hungry. My chest is doing something complicated—expanding and contracting at the same time—because I know what that word means. I know what comes before it.

"I didn't know." My voice comes out smaller than I intended.

"I don't talk about it much." He picks at his spring roll, not eating. "I was seven when I went into the system. Bounced around for a few years."

The system. Foster care. Group homes, maybe. The whole rotating door of adults who are supposed to be temporary but feel permanent when you're a kid trying to figure out why no one wants to keep you.

I know that door. I've spun through it myself.

"What happened to your parents? The first ones, I mean."

"My father left before I could remember him. My mother had problems she couldn't fix." He says it flatly, the way you describe something you've processed into scar tissue. "She tried. But trying wasn't enough to keep me fed or safe. CPS showed up, and I didn't see her again."

My throat tightens. The parallels are hitting too close, and I don't know what to do with my hands or the sudden urge to crawl into his lap and hold onto him like we're both still those kids who learned too early that love comes with an expiration date.

"Sebastian..."

"Eleanor was my fifth placement." He finally looks at me, and there's something raw in his expression. "I showed up with a chip on my shoulder the size of Manhattan. I wouldn't look at her. Wouldn't talk. I sat in the corner of my room and read for three weeks straight."

"Testing her."

"Yeah." His mouth curves, but it's not quite a smile. "I was waiting for her to decide I was too much trouble, like everyone else had."

Too much trouble. Too much work. The phrases are different, but the message is the same.

"What made her different?"

"She didn't give up." He says it simply, like it's obvious, but I can hear the wonder underneath, the part of him that still can't believe it. "I pushed. She stayed. I acted out. She stayed. I told her I hated her and she was ruining my life." A real smile now, rueful and warm. "She made me a grilled cheese sandwich and told me she'd be there when I was done being angry."

My eyes are burning. Goddammit. I just finished crying. I don't have the hydration reserves for more tears.

"When I was twelve, I went downstairs one morning and asked if I could stay permanently." He shakes his head, like he still finds it funny. "She laughed at me. Told me she'd been planning to ask me the same thing. The adoption was finalized shortly after that."

"Sebastian." His name comes out cracked in the middle.

"She taught me what it looks like to choose someone." He reaches across the takeout containers and takes my hand. His thumb traces my knuckles. "To pay attention. To stay when it would be easier to leave. She's the reason I know how to do this."

This. Us. Taking care of me when I fall apart. Remembering the coconut soup and the coffee preferences and the thousand tiny details that make up a person.

"I'd like you to meet her sometime. When you're ready."

The words hit like a wave I wasn't braced for. Meet the woman who taught him how to love.

"I'd like that," I manage.

He lifts my hand and kisses my palm. "No pressure. Whenever you're ready."

We sit in the quiet for a while, Thai food cooling between us. He gets me in a way no one else ever has. Not because we're the same—we're not—but because we both know what it's like to be the kid nobody wanted to keep.

And now he's here. Keeping me.

We watch randomly chosen comedy movies after lunch. My head ends up in his lap somewhere during the second one, his fingers combing through my hair in slow, repetitive strokes that make my whole body go liquid. I fall asleep during the third movie and wake up to find he's covered me with a blanket and is reading something on his tablet, his free hand still resting on my shoulder like he can't stand to not be touching me.

"I can go home," I mumble, still half-asleep. "You probably have stuff to do."

He gives me a soft smile. "I'm doing exactly what I want to do."

I don't know how to argue with that, so I close my eyes and let myself believe him.

When I wake up Monday morning, I'm feeling steadier. "I can go to work," I tell him over coffee, surprised to find it's true. "I want to."

He studies me for a long moment. "You're sure?"

"I'm sure." I set down my mug. "We can't stay here forever, as tempting as that sounds."

"The offer stands." His mouth quirks. "Permanent couch privileges. Unlimited Thai food. Me, in sweatpants, at your service."

I imagine him servicing me sexually in just his sweatpants, and my body perks up. Oh yeah, I'm feeling better.

"Careful. I might take you up on that someday."

He winks at me. "I'm counting on it."

Monday work is...fine. Good, even. Sebastian's gaze tracks me whenever we're in the same room, like he can't help himself. There's a thrilling tenderness in his expression when no one else is looking.

Every time I shift in my chair, echoes of the weekend make themselves known. The soreness in my ass. The faint marks hidden beneath my blouse where his mouth marked skin that no one else will ever see.

He's a possessive bastard. And I love it.

I also can't stop texting him.

It starts innocently enough. A thank you for the weekend. A comment about a meeting. But by lunch, I've devolved into a shameless slut.

Elise: I can't stop thinking about Saturday night.

Elise: I keep getting distracted thinking about you breeding me.

His response comes thirty seconds later.

Sebastian: You're playing a dangerous game, Ms. Hart.

Elise: Maybe I like danger.

Sebastian: Keep texting me like this and you'll find out exactly how much danger you're in.

My thighs clench under my desk. Very professional. I send back a single emoji—the innocent angel—and spend the next hour pretending to focus on spreadsheets while my pussy stages a mutiny.

By three o'clock, I've graduated to explicitly telling him exactly how much I need his cum. By four, I've described in detail what I want him to do about it. By five, I've abandoned all pretense of dignity and told him I'm wet just thinking about him bending me over his desk.

While I'm trying to tempt Sebastian to demand I come to his office, Tessa stops by my desk. "Hey, ready to head out for drinks?"

Oh yeah, the drinks. Dammit.

"Yeah, let me see if Sebastian is coming."

I pick up my phone to text him again, and Tessa laughs. "He has a late call. He said for us to have fun without him."

Double dammit. I was already planning how to torture him under the table. I turn my computer off and gather my purse. Sebastian texts me before we head out.

Sebastian: You're going to pay for every single one of these messages. Think of that while you're enjoying the drinks.

I'd be sad if I wasn't.

Elise: Promises, promises.

Fifteen minutes later, I'm wedged into a corner booth at a bar with Tessa, Daniel, and Cora, nursing my second glass of wine while they argue about a deal from 2019.

"—and I told him the EBITDA margins were garbage," Cora is saying, gesturing with her cocktail. "But did anyone listen to the analyst? No. Of course not."

"You were twenty-six." Daniel sips his whiskey. "And you delivered that assessment by literally throwing the report across the table."

"It got attention."

Tessa catches my eye and grins. "She's been impossible ever since Sebastian promoted her."

"I was impossible before that," Cora corrects. "The promotion gave me permission."

They pull me into the conversation naturally, like I've always been a part of their team. They ask my opinion on acquisition strategies and laugh at my jokes. Cora refills my wine without asking if I want more.

I always want more. They've figured this out. Which means they're paying attention. Which means they might actually like me.

"Sebastian was right about you," Daniel says during a lull. His eyes are kind. "Best strategic mind he's seen in a decade. And that's not praise he gives lightly."

My throat tightens.

"We're glad you're here, Elise." Tessa squeezes my hand across the table. "You fit."

"Welcome to the family," Daniel adds, clinking his glass against mine.

Family.

Sitting here, listening to Cora and Daniel bicker while Tessa rolls her eyes, I think I understand what it might feel like to belong.

My phone buzzes.

Sebastian: Come to my place when you're done. I've been thinking about your body all day. About all the things I haven't done to you yet.

Heat floods through me so fast I nearly choke on my wine. My pussy clenches around nothing, already on board with whatever he's planning.

Tessa catches my expression and smirks like she knows exactly what's happening on my screen.

"Tell Sebastian we said hi."

I don't bother denying it.

Twenty minutes later, I'm stepping out of the elevator into his condo, heart hammering against my ribs.

Things I haven't done to you yet.

What does that mean? We've done a lot. What's left? My brain supplies several extremely detailed suggestions, each more depraved than the last. My pussy votes yes to all of them without reading the fine print. Very responsible decision-making happening in my body right now.

He's waiting by the windows in a charcoal sweater and dark jeans. The city glitters behind him like a backdrop he commissioned personally. My boyfriend is hot.

Yeah, I've decided he's my boyfriend. I'm owning it.

When he turns, his gaze moves over me slowly, taking inventory. My nipples tighten under his attention like they're trying to get called on in class.

"Come here."

I cross to him. He doesn't touch me yet, lets the anticipation build in the space between us until my skin prickles with awareness. I want to beg him to touch me.

But I'm not going to beg. Yet. Give it five minutes.

"How are you feeling?"

"Better. Steady." I hold his gaze. "Ready."

His hand comes up to cup my jaw, tilting my face toward him. "You're sure? We don't have to—"

"Sebastian." I cover his hand with mine. "Shut up and fuck me."

His expression shifts to hunger, and he takes my hand, leading me to the bedroom.

When we're in the room, he faces me. "Take off your clothes."

The command slides through me, and my hands obey. As I remove my clothes, his eyes track every reveal like he's memorizing me for later reference.

By the time I'm standing in nothing but my bra and underwear, my pulse is racing.

"All of it."

I unclasp my bra and let it fall before hooking my thumbs in my panties and sliding them down.

His gaze is consuming. "On the bed. Hands above your head."

I move to his bedroom, hyperaware of his footsteps behind me. The sheets are cool against my bare skin as I stretch out, arms extended toward the headboard.

My pussy has been wet all day. She's an overachiever.

Sebastian stands at the foot of the bed, watching me like he's planning sweet, sweet torture for all my texts earlier.

It's time to tell him I'm on the pill. My heart is attempting a prison break through my ribs.

"I need to tell you something before we do anything."

His eyebrow rises. "Yes?"

I push up on my elbows so I can see his face clearly. "I did something last week."

"What do you mean?"

Oh god. Suddenly, I'm afraid of how he's going to react. Maybe I should have told him I wanted to do this? What if it's too fast? What if this freaks him out and he thinks I want him to actually breed me for real, and this sends him running? What if he does that thing where his face goes carefully blank and he says something reasonable that actually means *you've made a terrible miscalculation and now I need to figure out how to let you down easy*?

My brain offers a helpful highlight reel of Sebastian backing away slowly. *That's presumptuous.* Or worse, kind but distant. *I think we should talk about expectations.* Or the nuclear option: *I don't see this going in that direction.*

My hands are shaking. Great. Very seductive. I need to just get this over with.

I speak in a rush. "I went to the clinic and got tested. I'm clean. And I started the pill last week. It's been long enough to be effective."

Sebastian goes very still.

"I want your cum." The words tumble out before I can overthink them more than I already have. "Actually feel you inside me. Nothing between us."

This conversation was sexier in my head instead of this rushed, breathless mess. I'm really nailing this whole seduction thing.

I hold his gaze even though maintaining eye contact is one of the hardest things I've done recently. Including crying into his chest for forty-five minutes. "I want you inside me, bare."

For a long moment, he doesn't move. Doesn't speak.

The silence stretches. One second. Two. My brain kicks into overdrive. This was stupid. This was so stupid. I should get up before he kicks me out—

He snaps. Two strides, and he's on the bed, hauling me against him. His mouth takes mine like he's been holding back for weeks and the leash just broke. The kiss is feral. Consuming.

Oh.

Oh.

Not the nuclear option. The opposite of the nuclear option.

"I'm clean too," he says against my lips, voice rough. "Tested before our first time together."

"Then why aren't you fucking me yet?"

His eyes are dark pools of lust, and his voice is wrecked. "Jesus Christ, Elise."

He sits up and strips off his clothes. I've never seen someone get naked so fast. His cock is rock hard and straining towards me.

My body is basically chanting *yes yes yes* while my brain tries to process that this is actually happening.

He doesn't give me time to think. One second, he's kneeling on the bed; the next, he's pinning me to the mattress. His mouth crashes into mine like he's been starving for weeks and I'm the only thing that will save him. The kiss is brutal. Desperate. His teeth catch my lower lip, and I moan loudly.

He growls against my lips, and then he's shoving my thighs apart, settling between them, the head of his cock notching against my entrance.

No teasing. No slow buildup. Just raw, urgent need.

"Sebastian—"

He drives into me with one thrust. I cry out from the stretch and the overwhelming sensation of him bare inside me for the first time. I can feel *everything*. Every ridge, every pulse, every inch of him buried deep.

"Fuck." His voice is a growl that is barely human. "You feel—*fuck*—"

He doesn't wait for me to adjust. His hips snap back and slam forward again, setting a brutal pace that steals my breath. This isn't making love. This isn't even fucking. This is claiming.

And I love it.

"Yes!" I'm gasping, clawing at his shoulders, wrapping my legs around his hips to pull him deeper. "God, yes, harder!"

He gives me harder. Each thrust punches a sound out of me—moans, whimpers, desperate nonsense. The headboard cracks against the wall, and all I can do is hold on while he fucks me harder than he ever has.

"Mine," he snarls against my throat. "This pussy is *mine*."

"Yours." I can barely form words. "All yours."

"I'm going to fill you up." His pace is relentless. "Going to come so deep inside you, you feel it for days."

"Please." I'm already close to falling apart. "Please, I want it, I want to feel you."

He shifts his angle and hits a spot that makes my toes curl. My back arches off the bed as my nails sink into his shoulders.

"There?" He does it again. And again. Grinding against that spot with every stroke. "Right there?"

"Yes—fuck—don't stop—"

I come so hard I forget English. Forget my own name. Forget everything except the brutal pulse of pleasure and the way my body locks around him like it's trying to keep him forever. Sounds come out of my mouth—his name, maybe, or just vowels. Could be a prayer. Could be profanity. No way to tell.

He doesn't stop.

He fucks me through it, his cock dragging against my oversensitive walls, turning the aftershocks into continuous pleasure.

"One," he counts against my ear. "That's one."

Oh god.

"Sebastian, I can't—"

"You can." He pulls out suddenly and flips me onto my stomach like I weigh nothing. "Up. On your knees."

I scramble to obey, barely coordinated, my arms shaking as I push up onto all fours. He doesn't give me time to steady myself before he's slamming back into me from behind.

"*Fuck!*" I cry out as he sets a ruthless pace. The angle is deeper, and I swear I can feel him in my throat.

His hand fists in my hair, pulling my head back. His other hand grasps my hip, holding me in place.

"Is this what you wanted?" His voice is gravel. "Did you want me to fuck you raw? Fill you with my cum?"

"Yes!" I'm pushing back to meet every thrust, greedy and shameless. "Yes, breed me."

The words snap something in him. He goes harder. Faster. The sound of skin slapping skin fills the room. It's obscene and perfect. His cock is hitting places I didn't know existed, and I can feel another orgasm building impossibly fast.

"You want my cum that bad?" He yanks my hair harder, and I moan. "Want me to put a baby in you?"

"Yes—" I don't even know what I'm saying anymore. "Want it—want you to fill me up—please—"

"Such a good little slut." His hand leaves my hip and reaches around to find my clit. "Begging me to breed her."

The combination of his cock pounding into me and his fingers on my clit is too much. I come again. My arms give out, and my face smashes into the pillow as I scream through the waves of pleasure.

"Two." He groans. "Give me one more."

"I can't." I'm shaking, overstimulated, tears pricking at my eyes. "It's too much."

"You can take it." He pulls out and flips me again so I'm on my back, and he hauls my legs over his shoulder. I'm nearly folded in half. "You're going to take everything I give you."

He drives into me with long strokes that make my whole body jolt. There's sweat on his brow, and an absolute feral need in his eyes. He's barely holding on.

"Look at me while I fuck you," he demands.

I hold his gaze, and the room spins from delight.

"This pussy belongs to me." Each word is punctuated by a thrust. "Say it."

"Yours—" I'm sobbing now, overwhelmed. "My pussy is yours—"

"And when I come inside you—" He's losing rhythm, getting desperate. "When I fill you up, who does that cum belong to?"

"Me—" I'm clenching around him as another orgasm builds. "It's mine—I want it—please, Sebastian, give it to me."

"Beg me." His thumb presses hard against my clit. "Beg me to breed you."

"Please, please, please." I'm past pride, past shame, past anything except need. "Breed me, give me all your cum. I need it. Please!"

He slams deep and loses control, jackhammering into me as he chases his release. The pressure on my clit and the feeling of him swelling inside me pushes me over the edge one more time. I come screaming, clamping down on him so hard he groans.

"*Fuck.*"

He buries himself to the hilt as hot pulses of cum flood me—spurt after spurt while my pussy milks him through it. He keeps grinding into me like he's trying to push it further inside.

"Take it," he's muttering against my throat, still twitching inside me. "Every fucking drop."

Tears are sliding down my face because my body can't handle this. Three orgasms back to back, and I'm completely overwhelmed.

He finally goes limp against me, and we're both gasping and shaking.

Sebastian lifts his head and sees my tears. His expression of concern cuts through the post-orgasm haze.

"Hey." He brushes the wetness from my cheeks. "Too much?"

"No." I shake my head, laughing weakly. "It was perfect. I'm just...broken. You broke me."

Relief floods his face, followed by pure masculine satisfaction. "Good."

He pulls out slowly, and I gasp at the rush of his cum sliding down to pool beneath me. There's so much of it. I can feel it coating my thighs and dripping onto the sheets.

Sebastian looks down at the mess between my legs and makes a sound that's almost a growl. Before I can react, he's pushing through the wetness with his fingers, scooping his cum back up and pressing it inside me again.

"Sebastian," I moan and twitch from oversensitivity.

His voice is rough. Possessive. "You said it was yours. I'm keeping it inside you."

"That's not—" I'm trying to think through the mental fuzziness. "That's not how anatomy works—"

"Don't care." He slides two fingers deep, curling them, making me whimper. "I want to keep my cum inside you."

"You're insane."

"About you?" He finally withdraws his fingers and pulls me against his chest, not caring that we're both a mess. "Absolutely."

I lie there, shell-shocked and satisfied, trying to remember how to breathe. My pussy won't stop throbbing, and my thighs shake uncontrollably. His sheets are definitely getting washed after this, and I couldn't care less.

"That was..." I trail off, not sure how to finish.

"Yeah." He kisses the top of my head. "It was."

"I thought you were going to make me pay for my text messages."

"That was before *someone* said they got on the pill and begged for my cum." His hand traces lazy patterns on my spine. "I had a plan. A whole seduction scene with candles. That plan disintegrated the second you said the word 'bare.'"

"So what I'm hearing is I have power over you."

"Devastating amounts." He tips my chin up to kiss me softly. "I'd burn down the world if you asked."

"I'll keep that in mind."

We're silent for a moment. I can feel his cum still leaking out of me, and there's an odd rightness to it. I'm his.

"How do you feel?" he finally asks.

"Like I got fucked into another dimension." I press my face into his chest. The complicated answer can wait. Right now, I'm boneless and warm and full of him, and that's enough.

His laugh rumbles through me. "That was the goal."

My body hums with satisfaction as we snuggle together. I didn't know he'd react that way to me going on the pill, but it was pretty damn fabulous.

We're both quiet, lost in thoughts, until he says, "I want you to stay tonight."

"I wasn't planning on leaving."

His arms tighten around me, and for the first time in my life, I get it. This is what belonging feels like.

I wait for the doubts to start. For my brain to catalog everything that could go wrong. But my head stays quiet. There's only a strange new feeling that feels dangerously close to love.

I'm almost asleep when he speaks again.

"There's something I want to show you. Something I've been waiting on for the right time."

"Mmm?" I'm too boneless to form real words.

"I think you'll like it."

"Okay, but maybe after I sleep." My eyes are already closing. I'm not even sure the words come out right.

CHAPTER 13

I fell asleep.

He said he wanted to show me something, and I fell asleep like some kind of sex-drunk idiot before I could find out what.

Now it's Tuesday, and I'm staring at the Nelson proposal I stopped being able to read twenty minutes ago. Three hundred employees. Eighteen-month integration timeline. Org charts that need to merge without destroying either team's productivity. Patricia Nelson turned down two buyers already; if my strategy doesn't convince her we'll protect what she built, she'll walk again.

There's a solution here. I just haven't found it yet.

My brain doesn't want to work. It just keeps running scenarios about whatever Sebastian wanted to show me before I passed out. I'm a woman who has been edged and fucked into another dimension, so what hasn't he shown me? I've seen his playroom. What's left?

My imagination supplies options. Suspension rigging. Blindfolds. My thighs press together under my desk, and I realize I've been chewing my pen cap for ten minutes.

Senior Analyst of the Year material, right here.

The conference room empties after the integration review. I'm still riding the small high of watching the CFO's expression shift when I flagged the redundancy issue in Nelson's ops structure—parallel operations for the first year instead of an immediate merge. It'll cost more upfront but protect productivity during transition.

"That was sharp thinking, Hart," Daniel says as he passes my chair. "The parallel ops angle. Patricia Nelson will like that."

I try not to glow visibly. Validation from Daniel is rare.

I'm gathering my notes when Sebastian's hand closes around my elbow.

"Come with me."

It's not a request. My clit gives a little salute of acknowledgment. *Down, girl. We're at work. Have some dignity.* Not that she ever cares.

He steers me out of the conference room, down the hall, and before I can process what's happening, he opens a supply closet door and pulls me inside.

The door shuts and there's total darkness except for a sliver of light under the door. Shelves of printer paper and toner cartridges. The smell of cardboard and—

His mouth crashes into mine.

I make a sound that would be embarrassing if I had any brain cells left to feel embarrassment. He pulls me flush against him and I can feel how hard he is through his suit pants. The kiss is filthy—tongue and teeth and the kind of desperation that says he's been thinking about this all through the meeting.

When he pulls back, I'm panting. My panties, already a lost cause, have officially surrendered. They're waving the white flag and requesting evacuation.

"I told you I wanted to show you something." His voice is rough in the dark. "Tonight at my place. Be there at eight o'clock."

Oh. The mystery thing from last night. He dragged me into a supply closet to tell me this. My brain is still short-circuiting from the kiss, so I say the first thing that comes to mind.

"You could have woken me up last night."

"You were tired." I can hear the smile in his voice. "I'll forgive you. This time."

"How generous." I'm aiming for dry but it comes out breathless. "So? What is it?"

His hand finds my chin in the darkness, tilts my face up even though we can barely see each other. "You'll see."

His thumb traces my lower lip.

"Wear something easy to remove."

"Sir, I'm standing in a supply closet. Everything I'm wearing is easy to remove right now."

He just chuckles.

Yep, I'm going to walk out of this closet, sit through a 3 p.m. meeting, and pretend I'm a functioning adult and not soaking wet because my boss has kinky plans for me tonight.

This is a skill they didn't teach in business school.

The rest of the day drags. Every time I try to focus on reports, my mind wanders to tonight. My brain helpfully supplies a highlight reel of options, most of which would make a porn star raise an eyebrow.

Tessa catches me staring at my screen without blinking.

"You okay?"

"Fine. Great. Totally fine." I am a terrible liar. "Big project tonight."

She grins like she knows exactly what kind of project. "Have fun."

"It's not—we're—" I give up. "Thanks."

By the time I'm riding the elevator to his condo at 7:58, my nerves are singing. My skin feels too tight for my body. I've changed my panties three times after work—first to a sexy lace pair, then cotton, then nothing at all because Sebastian texted two hours ago: *No panties.* The bastard.

I'm so turned on I might combust the second he touches me. Just spontaneously orgasm in his doorway like some kind of feral cat in heat.

He's at the door when the elevator opens to his condo. Still in his work shirt and slacks, though he's unbuttoned enough to show his white undershirt. No shoes. He looks casual except for the heat in his eyes when he sees me.

His gaze drags down my body, lingering on the pink sundress, the heels I'm about ready to kick off.

"Come with me."

I ditch the heels, and he leads me down the hallway to the playroom. But instead of stopping at the main area, he guides me to the far wall, where a door blends almost invisibly into the charcoal paneling. I didn't notice it last time we were in here.

My pulse picks up. This is unknown territory. Either it's going to be incredible, or I'm going to discover he collects clown paintings or has a shrine to an ex-wife I don't know about, or worse.

He opens it.

The room is small with warm lighting. The only furniture is a low platform bed centered in the room with slate blue sheets.

And covering the entire far wall—floor to ceiling, corner to corner—is a mirror.

Oh.

Oh no.

Oh no no no.

That's a lot of mirror. That's so much mirror. That's enough mirror to show me every unflattering angle, every weird face I make, every jiggle and roll and—

"Sebastian..."

He steps behind me, hands settling on my hips. In the mirror, I see us: his head bent toward my ear, my eyes too wide, my chest rising faster.

"I want you to see what I see when you come."

Heat floods through me. My pussy clenches around nothing, apparently very on board with this plan. Yeah, I don't know...that's looking at the needy, desperate woman I become with him and losing the right to pretend she doesn't exist. Plausible deniability has been my friend. Mirrors are snitches.

"I don't know if I can."

"That's why we're going to try." His fingers play with the spaghetti straps of my sundress. "Color?"

"Green." My voice wavers. "Nervous green. Terrified green. Green mixed with wanting to bolt for the door."

He laughs. "If it becomes too much, we'll stop."

In one smooth motion, he grips the hem of my sundress and pulls it over my head. My bra is unhooked and discarded before I can take a full breath.

His eyes drop to my bare pussy, then back up to my face.

"Good girl."

My clit preens at the praise. She followed instructions. She's very obedient.

I'm completely naked now, and there's nowhere to hide. I stare at my reflection. At the flush creeping down my chest. At how hard my nipples are.

"Look at you." His voice is rough. "I barely touch you, and your whole body lights up."

"Sebastian—"

"Watch."

He's still behind me, and he slides a hand down my stomach. When he reaches my pussy, his fingers part my folds, and I see myself in the mirror—legs spreading for him automatically, hips tilting into his touch. I look wanton. Desperate. Like a woman who would do anything he asked.

"So wet already." He circles my clit, and I watch my own face twist with pleasure. Is that what I look like? Is that my mouth doing that?

"Did you touch yourself today?"

"No, Sir."

"Good girl." Two fingers sink inside me, and I moan as I watch them disappear. "You save this for me. This pretty pussy is all mine."

"All yours." I'm panting and rocking my hips against his hand. It's obscene watching myself fuck his fingers. It's also crazy hot. My brain wants to unpack why that is, but my body tells it to shut up and enjoy the show.

"Please—"

"Please what?" He curls his fingers, hitting that spot that makes stars burst behind my eyes. "Tell me what you want. And watch yourself ask for it."

I meet my own gaze in the mirror, taking in my flushed cheeks, parted lips, and glazed eyes.

The woman looking back at me doesn't seem like someone who would eat her birthday cupcake alone in a copier room. She looks like someone who knows exactly what she wants and isn't afraid to ask for it.

Maybe that's who I'm becoming.

"I want you to fuck me." The words sound like they're coming from that confident woman in the mirror. "I want to watch you fuck me. I want to see your cock inside me."

His groan vibrates against my neck. "Get on the bed. Hands and knees. Face the mirror."

I climb onto the platform, positioning myself so I'm staring straight at my own reflection. The angle is devastating; I can see everything. My breasts hanging heavy, swaying slightly. My spine curved. My ass raised and waiting.

Behind me, Sebastian strips quickly. I watch his cock spring free, thick and hard, and my pussy clenches. She's ready. She's been ready since this morning. Possibly since the moment I met him.

"Don't look away." He kneels behind me on the bed. "I want you to see everything I do to you."

He grasps my hips, and I feel the blunt head of his cock nudging my entrance, and—he doesn't push in. The tip barely breaches before retreating. Teasing.

No. No no no. He can't do this to me. He can't just—

"Sebastian—"

Another short thrust, another withdrawal before I can take more.

My body is screaming. My pussy is trying to drag him in through sheer force of will, clenching around nothing, desperate for more than this maddening almost. My face in the mirror is needy and desperate.

"Please, I need—" I try to push back against him, but his grasp on my hips tightens as he holds me still. "—please—"

"Watch yourself beg." His voice is strained. "Look at the eager slut in the mirror."

I'm a flushed and panting mess. I'm ready to promise him anything—my 401k, my firstborn, my soul—if he'll just *fuck me.*

"Please, please, fuck me, oh god—" The words come out broken.

He slams in.

One long stroke that fills me completely. We both groan when he bottoms out.

In the mirror, I watch his fingers dig into my hips. Watch my own face as I feel every bare inch of his cock inside me.

"Fuck," he growls. "Look at how sexy you are."

I can't look away from the obscene image of my breasts swaying with each thrust. My mouth falls open on sounds I can't control.

My vision goes fuzzy as the sensations build. The woman in the mirror looks drunk on pleasure.

His hand fists in my hair, pulling my head up when I start to drop. "Eyes on the mirror."

"I can't—" He thrusts hard, and my words scatter. "It's too—oh god—"

"You can." Another thrust. "You will." Another. "Watch yourself take my cock like a good girl." His hips slam against my ass. "Watch yourself"—thrust—"fall apart"—thrust—"for me."

The pleasure is building fast, coiling tight in my core. But it's more than physical; it's seeing myself like this. Seeing the woman I become with him. I'm oddly beautiful in my surrender.

"Sebastian—I'm going to—"

"Not yet." He pulls out, and I whimper. "Turn over onto your back."

I collapse onto my back, legs shaking, and he's on me immediately, spreading my thighs, settling between them, pushing back inside in one smooth stroke. The new angle makes me gasp.

"Turn your head." His voice is rough. "Watch."

I turn toward the mirror and—oh. *Oh.*

From here I can see everything. His hips between my spread thighs. His cock sliding in and out of me, glistening with my arousal.

"I want to fill you first." He rolls his hips slowly, keeping me right on the edge. "I want you to watch me come inside you."

The words arrow straight to my clit. "Please."

"Tell me what you want." His hand wraps around my throat, not squeezing. Claiming. "Say it while you look yourself in the eye."

I stare at my reflection. At the woman with her hair wild, throat circled by his hand, body impaled on his cock.

"I want you to come inside me." My voice is raw, and I don't break eye contact with myself. "I want to watch you breed me."

"Jesus Christ." His control snaps.

He fucks me hard and fast, cock driving so deep I can't do anything but cling to his shoulders and hang on. I watch the tension in his face in the mirror, the moment he finally lets go and buries himself to the hilt.

He explodes, and I feel it. Hot pulses of cum flood my pussy. Spurt after spurt, filling me up until I'm overflowing.

"Now." His fingers rub quick circles on my clit. "Be a good girl and come for me."

My whole body seizes, clenching around his cock so hard I'm surprised he doesn't yelp. In the mirror, I watch my face contort into something unrecognizable, watch my mouth open on a scream I can't hear over the blood rushing in my ears.

It doesn't stop. His fingers on my clit drag it out, wave after wave, until I'm not sure where one orgasm ends and the next begins.

When it finally subsides, I'm shaking. Tears track down my face, and I don't know when that started.

Sebastian pulls out slowly. I feel the rush of his cum following, sliding down my inner thighs.

"Wait a minute."

He moves from between my legs and repositions me before I can process what's happening. He turns me so my back rests against a pillow, thighs spread wide. I'm facing the mirror directly.

"Now look."

Between my spread legs, I can see everything. My swollen, reddened pussy. The white cum dripping from my hole, trailing down toward the sheets. The evidence of what he did. What I let him do. What I begged for.

He settles beside me, propped on one elbow, watching my face as his fingers trace through the mess. He gathers his cum and pushes it back inside me.

"So beautiful filled with my cum." He watches my face in the mirror as he fucks his cum back into me with two fingers. "This pretty pussy. This body. You. All of it belongs to me."

"Yes." I can barely speak. "Yours."

"And this—" He pulls his hand from my pussy and lays his palm against my lower belly. "Someday you'll really be carrying my baby."

Fuck, he knows exactly what to say to turn me into a puddle.

"But for now..." He settles beside me and pulls me close, tucking me against his chest until we're curved together, his body wrapped around mine. I'm the little spoon, and we're facing the mirror. "I want to just enjoy you."

We make a debauched picture in the mirror. Tangled together, slick with sweat and cum, flushed and thoroughly relaxed.

"I can't believe I look like that," I whisper.

"Like what?"

"So satisfied. Happy." The words feel strange in my mouth. "Like I actually enjoy my life."

He kisses my shoulder. "You do look happy."

I giggle and watch the woman in the mirror smile back at me. She looks soft. Glowing. "I don't even recognize that woman." I study her for another moment. She's smiling and fits against him without tension. "But I like her. I think she might be the real me."

He hums softly and kisses my hair. "She's definitely the real you. And she's magnificent."

That weird feeling that borders on love washes over me again, warm and terrifying and too big to name. I whisper, "You're pretty magnificent too."

I'm not ready to examine what any of this means or where this is going, so I close my eyes and let myself be held. For now, this is enough.

Later, I'm wrapped in his robe, sitting at his kitchen island while he stirs a pot on the stove. My body is pleasantly sore, thoroughly used, and I can still feel the ghost of him between my legs.

"Is that...mac and cheese? From a box?"

He doesn't look up. "Yep, problem?"

"No, I just—" I bite back a grin. "I expected your post-sex meal to be, I don't know, truffle risotto. Wagyu sliders. Something with foam."

"Hey, this is the fancy mac and cheese." He waves the box at me. "Real sauce in a foil packet. None of that powder crap. We're nothing but high class around here."

I snort. Somehow, this is better. More real. Sebastian Ashford, CEO, stirring neon orange pasta in a pot like a college student. For me.

After we eat, we snuggle on the couch. I'm half-melted against him when his hand stills on my back. "There's something we need to discuss." His tone turns serious. "Something at work."

The shift in tone makes me straighten.

Uh-oh. Is this the part where he tells me HR has concerns. Is the other shoe finally going to drop and crush everything I've let myself want?

"What is it?"

"It's about Lydia."

My immediate relief almost makes me giggle, which is soooo not an appropriate response right now.

He continues. "I traced that text. It was sent from a burner app, but IT confirmed the originating device was registered to her home network."

Oh.

Oh, that's actually worse than HR concerns. My stomach twists into a knot, then twists again for good measure.

"So what happens now?"

"HR is investigating. But she's been asking questions at work—about your promotion, your access levels." He meets my eyes. "I wanted you to know what we're dealing with."

The words echo in my skull, spawning scenarios like rabbits. Lydia with photos. Lydia with audio recordings. Lydia compiling a detailed timeline of every time I've been in his office with the door locked. Did she see us in the supply closet? The parking garage? Maybe she planted a spy cam in his office, and she's got screenshots and timestamps with my face frozen mid-orgasm.

"So what do we do?"

"For now? Nothing different. You earned your position. Your work speaks for itself." He tips my chin up with one finger. "But I wanted you to know. No secrets between us."

"No secrets," I agree.

But even as I say it, dread coils tight in my gut. Lydia's been watching. She's planning something.

Sebastian kisses my forehead, and I try to let his steadiness calm me.

It doesn't work.

Chapter 14

Two days after Sebastian tells me that Lydia is asking questions, I'm summoned to the conference room for a meeting. When the elevator doors open on the executive floor, I know immediately that I'm walking into a disaster.

Not because of anything specific, but because of the silence. The three guys standing by the elevator stop talking as soon as they see me. Conversations die as I pass. People step aside without looking at me directly, like I've become contagious overnight.

Oh yeah. This meeting is about me.

The thought lands like a punch to the solar plexus. Is it too late to call in sick? I could flee to Canada and start over as a sheep farmer in Nova Scotia. Sheep don't care about office politics. Sheep don't give a shit about whatever's waiting for me in that conference room.

My body has decided to break out in stress sweat under my silk blouse. Very professional.

The conference room doors loom at the end of the hallway. My feet keep moving even though every survival instinct I've ever developed is screaming at me to run.

I push open the door, and twelve faces turn toward me. The room falls silent. Lydia Kessler is seated at the far end with a folder in front of her. She looks like a cat that's cornered a mouse and she's been waiting for this moment.

Photographs are spread across the polished conference table. My stomach knots. This is it, the moment of exposure and humiliation. It's the inevitable fall.

"Ah, Ms. Hart." Lydia's voice is honey poured over razor blades. "Perfect timing. I was just sharing some documentation with everyone."

Don't look at the photos. Don't look at the photos. Don't—

I look at the photos.

The nearest one is me leaving Sebastian's building at dawn. Then there's the two of us in his car, his profile unmistakable, while I lean toward him in a way that makes it obvious we're about to kiss.

"I have timestamps," Lydia says, and the satisfaction in her voice makes my blood run cold. "I have a detailed account of every time Ms. Hart entered or exited Mr. Ashford's private residence. She's been sleeping with him since before her promotion."

I mean, technically, he gave me the promotion and then I sucked his cock, but I don't think that's going to win me any points right now.

The room tilts. I'm floating somewhere near the ceiling, watching the version of me standing there and forgetting how to breathe. Twelve people are looking at those photos. Twelve people are imagining me being rewarded with a fancy title for being good at taking cock.

Everything I've done here, none of it will ever matter again.

"This company has ethics policies," Lydia says, and I can hear her distantly through the static. "Mr. Ashford's judgment is clearly compromised. The board should consider—"

"That's enough."

Sebastian's voice cuts through the fog as he walks into the room. He looks at Lydia with such coldness, I swear the temperature drops ten degrees.

"Ms. Kessler." He pauses next to me, every movement of his controlled. "You've just accused a colleague of professional misconduct based on photographs that prove nothing except that two consenting adults spend time together outside of work."

"The timeline—"

"The documentation will show that I emailed HR with the promotion request the day we took over the company. Did she have time to sleep her way to the top in a few hours?"

Lydia's face flushes an ugly, mottled red.

"Her performance reviews are impeccable. Her contributions to the integration strategy have been well documented." Sebastian's gaze sweeps the room, and I watch everyone shift like they're recalibrating. "If anyone here believes I would compromise this company's interests for a personal relationship, I invite you to review the numbers since Ms. Hart was promoted."

The look on everyone's face changes, like they're evaluating the situation instead of immediately damning me.

The legal department head clears his throat. "Sebastian's right. There's nothing here that violates company policy. Dating between colleagues isn't prohibited, and there's no evidence of favoritism."

"But—" Lydia starts.

"What I do see," he continues, his voice hardening, "is a senior manager using company time and resources to surveil a colleague. That concerns me significantly more."

I watch Lydia's face transform as she realizes what's happening. The blade she sharpened for weeks is now pointed at her own throat.

Sebastian's voice is quiet. "I think Ms. Kessler and I need to have a private conversation about her future with this company. Unless anyone has further questions?"

No one responds.

"Then this meeting is over."

I don't remember leaving the boardroom. One moment I'm standing frozen by the conference table, the next I'm in the bathroom, locked in a stall, on the floor with my knees pulled to my chest.

Every time I let myself hope. Every time I trusted someone enough to stop bracing for the impact...

The impact came anyway.

A sob tears out of me, then another. Within moments, I'm crying so hard I can't see, can't think, can't do anything except fall apart.

"Elise?" Tessa's voice is outside the stall.

My throat is sealed shut, and I can't answer.

"I saw you run in here. Let me in, please."

My hand moves without permission, flipping the lock. Tessa opens the door and takes one look at me—snot-faced, mascara destroyed—and crouches down.

"Look at me. Breathe. In through your nose, out through your mouth."

"She…" The words splinter. "Everyone saw—"

"I heard what happened." Tessa's jaw tightens. "Lydia's a bitch."

"I didn't sleep with him before—" A hiccup breaks through. "Before the promotion. She's wrong about that."

"Elise." Tessa grips my hands hard enough to ground me. "You're brilliant at your job. Everyone who's worked with you knows that. Sebastian doesn't give positions to people he's fucking. He gives them to people who deserve them. Lydia can spin whatever story she wants, but your work speaks for itself."

She hands me toilet paper for my face. I blow my nose so hard it echoes off the tile, which is exactly as glamorous as it sounds.

"They're going to remember Sebastian standing up in front of the entire board and defending you." Tessa's voice is soothing. "They're going to remember Lydia's face when she realized she'd overplayed her hand."

She pulls me into a hug that I wasn't expecting, and I don't know what to do.

"I'm getting snot on your blouse."

"I have three of this blouse. You're fine."

That gets a wet giggle from me, and I hug her back because apparently, I'm the kind of person who cries in bathrooms and hugs people now.

Tessa helps me up and I fix what's left of my makeup in the mirror. She doesn't say anything as she waits while I put myself back together piece by piece.

When she can tell I'm done, she asks, "You okay?"

"Yeah, I'm okay."

The word tastes like a lie. But I can't hide in this bathroom forever.

She squeezes my hand once, and we walk out together.

Two hours later, I watch from my desk as security escorts Lydia from the building. Her face is white with humiliation.

I expected to feel triumphant, but there's just a hollow pit in my stomach. I'm scraped clean like a pumpkin, all the guts removed and nothing left but rind.

Daniel appears at my side. "She was given the option to resign or face a formal investigation for workplace harassment and misuse of company resources. Sebastian gave her fifteen minutes to decide. She took three."

"She's really gone?"

"Yeah." He squeezes my shoulder. "And he wants to see you in his office."

Sebastian's door is open. He's standing by the window, jacket off, tie loosened, and when I step inside, he turns with an expression that cracks me open all over again.

"Close the door."

Once it's closed, he looks at me for a long moment, reading my face. Then he crosses the room and pulls me against his chest so hard I lose my breath.

"I'm sorry." His voice is rough against my hair. "I should have seen this coming and protected you better."

"You couldn't have known she was going to do that."

"I knew she was up to something." His arms tighten. "I should have dealt with her before she had a chance to hurt you."

I pull back enough to see his face. The guilt there catches me off guard—this man who controls everything thinks he should have done more.

"You stood up in front of the entire company." My voice comes out hoarse. "You defended me."

"You were still hurt." His hands frame my face. "I'm supposed to protect you."

My eyes are burning. I will not cry again. A tear escapes anyway. Stupid eyes.

"Everyone knows." The words stick in my throat. "Everyone saw those photos."

"Yes." He kisses my forehead. "Does that change things for you?"

"Does it change things for you?"

"Elise." His voice drops and goes dark in a way that sends heat curling through my belly despite everything. "I stood up in front of the department heads and essentially declared that you're mine. What do you think?"

The possessiveness reaches past the shame and the exposure.

"I think..." I swallow. "I think I need you to take me home and remind me who I belong to."

His eyes glitter. "Yeah?"

"Everyone knows now." I grip his shirt, pulling him closer. "And I want you to fuck me until I can't think about anything except you inside me."

The growl he makes isn't human.

It's not even five o'clock, and we leave together. We barely make it to his condo.

His mouth is on mine before the elevator closes. Hands drag my blouse from my skirt, buttons scattering across the marble floors. I'm clawing at his shirt, desperate for skin, desperate to erase the last few hours with contact that proves I'm still his.

"Bedroom," he groans against my throat.

"Too far." I yank his belt open and shove his pants down.

He spins me around and bends me over the arm of the couch. My skirt gets shoved up around my waist, and he slides his hand between my thighs.

Satisfaction roughens his voice. "Already dripping for me."

"Please." I push back against him. "Please, I need you."

My panties rip, and I gasp as his fingers slide through my folds, spreading my wetness.

"What do you need?" He circles my clit once before pulling away. "Tell me."

"Your cock." The words come out broken. "I need your cock."

He notches himself at my entrance and presses forward just enough for me to feel the stretch. Then stops.

"Sebastian!"

"Who do you belong to?" He rocks against me in shallow, teasing thrusts. It's not nearly enough.

"You. I belong to—please—"

Another press forward, giving me an inch. My pussy clenches around him.

"The entire board knows now." He slides in a little more, and I moan. "Everyone in the building knows you're mine."

"Yes."

"And you still want this?" He pulls out and then gives me just the tip again. "Do you still want me to own you? Fuck you? Fill you up until you're dripping with my cum?"

"Oh god, yes, please." I start babbling incoherently. I can hear myself making sounds that would be embarrassing if I had any dignity left, but I don't. I spent it all crying in the bathroom, and now I'm bent over a couch begging him to fuck me. "Please, I need you, I can't—"

He slams into me in one brutal thrust, and I cry out in pleasure.

He fucks me hard and fast, driving so deep I have to cling to the couch to stop myself from flying off. This isn't the controlled dominance of the playroom.

"Mine." He punctuates the word with a thrust that makes colors explode behind my eyes. "This pussy is mine."

"Yours!"

"This body." Another brutal stroke. "Your mouth." His hand slides around to my throat, gripping, but not pressing down. "This fucking heart."

"Yes. God, yes." The pressure on my neck makes me needier. "All of it. All—"

"Everyone knows." He lets go of my throat and fucks me harder. "Everyone in that boardroom saw me claim you. And I'd do it again in front of a hundred people. A thousand."

I'm close. The sheer filthy possessiveness of his words is pushing me toward the edge.

He snakes a hand down between my legs and rubs my clit as he fucks me. Within seconds, the orgasm rips through me. I'm chanting, "Oh god," as I convulse around him, clenching and writhing while he fucks me through it.

"Good girl." His voice is strained. "Squeeze my cock and show me how much you love being owned."

"Please—" I don't know what I'm begging for anymore. "Sebastian, please—"

"Want me to fill you up?" He slams in deep, grinding against my ass. "Remind you who you belong to with my cum?"

"Yes. Yes. Yes!"

He groans loudly, and I feel the hot pulse of cum flooding me. I'm suddenly coming again, squealing as I buck against him.

He keeps thrusting as he unloads deep inside me, refusing to let a single drop escape.

When he finally stills, we're both shaking. Yeah, he just fucked me silly.

He pulls out slowly, and his cum immediately drips down my thighs. He growls with satisfaction.

His hand presses against my lower back, keeping me bent over the couch. "Look at my cum leaking out."

I want to tell him I can't look at it, but I can only moan as his fingers slide into my pussy, finger fucking me slowly as if he's trying to push the cum back in.

"I'm going to keep you like this." He works two fingers deeper into me. "I want you full of me so you never forget."

"Couldn't forget." I whimper. "Not ever."

He withdraws his fingers and wipes them on my thigh. I shiver from how filthy this is, and he helps me up and holds me steady since my legs don't want to work.

When he turns me around, his tender expression makes my breath catch.

"Today didn't destroy us," he says quietly.

"No, it didn't."

"Because you're mine and I'm yours. There's nothing anyone can do about it."

I press my face into his shoulder, and he wraps his arms around me. Today was horrible, but his claiming me in front of everyone is what mattered.

Later, tangled together in his bed, I trace patterns on his chest. "What happens now? At work?"

"Now we're official." He catches my hand and kisses my fingers one by one. "HR wants us to sign some paperwork. Nothing that affects your position, just documentation of our relationship."

"And people will talk."

"People always talk." His arm tightens around me. "Let them. You earned your position. Anyone who suggests otherwise can answer to me."

"My protective CEO."

"Your protective everything." He tips my chin up for a slow kiss. "I'm sorry today happened, but I'm not sorry everyone knows. I was getting tired of pretending."

"Me too."

His smile warms me. This is the version of him only I get to see. I settle against his chest, letting his heartbeat steady me.

Tomorrow, there will be paperwork and gossip, plus probably more uncomfortable conversations than I can count. But right now, his arms are around me, and there's a quiet in my soul. It's a belief that maybe, just maybe, I've finally found where I belong.

CHAPTER 15

It's been three glorious weeks of being his and not hiding our feelings when we look at each other. Three weeks of spending time with him in the breakroom without having to be careful not to stand too close.

The whispers have mostly stopped, and Sebastian's hand on my lower back in meetings, visible and unapologetic, has shifted the narrative. Now it's not "she slept her way up," it's "he claimed her in front of everyone." I'm not sure which is worse, but I'm also not sure I care anymore.

The Nelson presentation is Friday. I've run through my slides forty times. On paper, it's solid. But in my head, Patricia Nelson is already ripping it apart and I'm crawling out of the conference room in humiliated pieces.

I'm trying to convince myself Friday will be fine while getting coffee in the breakroom when my phone lights up. Why is Sebastian calling me?

His voice is different when I answer. He's not using his commanding work voice. My pussy perks up hopefully, but it's not his sexy dom voice either. Down, girl. We're in public.

His voice is careful. "Come over for dinner tonight. I'm cooking."

"You're cooking?" My palms go damp. "Should I be worried? Is this a 'we need to talk' dinner?"

He pauses for way too long. "No."

"That's not reassuring."

"Dinner is at seven." His voice goes soft. "Trust me."

He hangs up before I can spiral out loud, but my brain doesn't need permission. The disasters queue up: he's bored and done with me. I'm too much work. I've been waiting for this moment since the first night I stayed over.

By the time the elevator opens into his condo, my legs are jelly and my reflection in the mirror on the wall looks slightly feral. This is definitely the face of a woman who is probably going to lose her cool when he breaks up with her.

When he walks out of the kitchen wearing jeans and a gray sweater, my insides go all soft and gooey. This is domestic Sebastian. The version of him that exists only in private.

He takes my hand. "Don't look so terrified."

"I'm not terrified." I'm vibrating with terror. "I'm cautiously anticipatory. It's nuanced."

He waits while I kick off my shoes and then leads me into the kitchen, where the scent of garlic and rosemary fills the air. He made spaghetti, and it's good, but my anxiety isn't letting me fully appreciate it.

He catches me pushing my food around the plate. "You've barely eaten."

"I'm savoring it."

"You're stressing."

"I can do both. I'm very talented."

He takes my hand and squeezes it, and doesn't press me to eat.

After the dishes are cleared, he leads me to the living room and settles me on the couch. He sits next to me, but he's not touching me.

"There's something I want to give you."

I blink. That's not the script I was expecting.

"It's something I've been thinking about for a while."

He reaches into the drawer of the side table and pulls out a long velvet box. I blink at it. He's giving me jewelry?

"I'd like to make this official." He says it fast, like he can see my brain short-circuiting in real time. "This is significant. To me. To what we are."

My heart gives a painful thud as he opens the box. Inside, resting on black velvet, is a delicate gold chain necklace. Dangling from it is a small, perfect lock. It's functional, and I can tell it will stay shut if it's closed.

My clit throbs, which is a weird response to jewelry, but apparently that's who I am now.

"This is a day collar." His voice is soft. "In my world, it means ownership and commitment. It's a promise that goes beyond anything we've done so far."

The gold catches the light, and I can't look away from it. He wants to make this official.

"I'm not asking you to wear it because you're my submissive." He tips my chin up to force me to look at him. "I'm asking you to wear it because you're *mine*. And I want you to carry a reminder of that."

"Sebastian..." I'm too shocked to think of a response.

"The lock has a key." He reaches into his pocket and pulls out his keyring. There's a tiny gold key on it. "I keep this. You can't take the necklace off without me."

This is a claim I'll wear constantly and removable only by him. Half of me is screaming *yes*. I'll have the reminder that I belong to him and that he wants to keep me.

The other half is telling me to think this through. Giving someone this much power to hurt me is dangerous. What happens if he leaves?

But I'm tired of letting fear make my decisions. And the yes is louder than it's ever been.

"In some relationships," he continues, and I notice a tremor in his hands as he holds the box, "a collar is almost like an engagement ring. It's a promise of permanence." His eyes search mine. "That's what I'm offering you, if you want me."

"You really want me?" I hate how small my voice sounds.

He takes my hands, and his warmth makes me realize my fingers are ice blocks. "I do, but this is about you choosing to be mine."

Me choosing. I look at the collar again. It's small enough to hide under a blouse and elegant enough to pass as jewelry to anyone who doesn't know.

"What happens if I say yes?"

"Then I put it on you, and you know you're mine."

He squeezes my hand in reassurance, and my pussy clenches like he just promised to fuck me. She's celebrating prematurely.

"And if I say no?"

"Then nothing changes, and we continue as we are. I'll be disappointed, but I'll understand." He brings my hands to his lips and kisses my palm. "This isn't an ultimatum. You can say no if it's too soon."

I think about everything that's happened since I met him. The negotiation where I sat across from him, pretending my panties weren't soaked. The first time he made me come so hard I forgot how to form words. The way he's broken me open and put me back together, over and over, until the woman who ate a birthday cupcake alone seems like a character from someone else's life.

I think about Lydia and the photographs. The conference room was full of people who saw Sebastian stand in front of them and claim me without hesitation.

"Yes." The word comes out steady. Which is honestly a miracle because my insides are vibrating.

"Yes?" His voice cracks.

"Yes, I want to be yours."

His face transforms. All the control vanishes, and what's left is exposed and so damn vulnerable my throat goes tight.

He takes the necklace from the box. "Turn around."

I turn and lift my hair, baring my neck. My hands are shaking and my heart is trying to break through my ribs.

He drapes the chain around my throat. The weight settles against my collarbone, and it's heavier than it looks. The click of the lock is quiet.

"There." His breath is warm against my ear. "You're mine now."

I'm wearing a literal lock around my neck, and somehow, this feels less trapped than I've ever felt in my entire life.

When I lower my hair and turn to face him, I'm not the same person I was five minutes ago. This new woman knows she's wanted.

"How does it feel?" he asks.

Simple words. Give him simple words.

"Like I'm yours." My voice barely makes it past my throat.

He kisses me softly. "I'm going to take you to bed now." He murmurs against my mouth. "And I'm going to fuck you while you wear my collar. So you understand exactly what it means to belong to me."

Heat floods through me. My pussy is already wet, and the promise in his voice makes it worse. "Yes, Sir."

He doesn't wait until we're in the bedroom to undress me. He walks me backwards, his mouth still on mine as he unbuttons my blouse. Then my skirt, his hands pushing it down over my hips, so I have to step out of it. My bra goes somewhere. By the time my back hits the bedroom doorframe, I'm in nothing but my panties and the collar around my throat.

"These"—his fingers hook into the waistband—"are ruined."

"It's your fault."

"Yes." He drags them down my legs and pauses when he sees exactly how wet I am. "It is."

I expect him to push me toward the bed, but he turns me around and presses me against the nearest wall. My breasts are smashed against the cool plaster, and his cock is hard and grinding against me through his slacks.

"Sebastian," I moan, trying to push my ass back for more friction.

"Stay still." His mouth finds the back of my neck, right where the collar chain sits.

I shiver and press my forehead against the wall. My nipples are hard and aching, and every breath scrapes them against the wall. My clit throbs in time with my pulse.

His hands skim down my hips and around my stomach.

"You're beautiful like this." His voice is rough. "Wearing my collar, naked and waiting for me to decide what happens next."

I'm breathless. "What happens next?"

"I'm going to tie you up." He bites the curve of my shoulder. "Then I'm going to make you come while wearing my collar."

Mmm, I like this plan.

He walks me to the bed and positions me on my back with my arms above my head. His eyes never leave mine as he strips—shirt, pants, boxer briefs—and god, his cock is so hard and thick. My mouth waters at the sight of it. I'm not sure I've ever seen him this hard. Clearly me wearing his collar makes his cock enthused.

He opens the nightstand and pulls out red rope. "I'm going to bind your wrists to remind you that you're not in control tonight."

"Yes, Sir."

He takes his time with it, wrapping the rope around my wrists and threading it through itself. He tests the tension, adjusting until it's tight enough to hold but not tight enough to hurt me. When he's done, my arms are stretched above me, secured to the headboard, and I'm completely open.

Completely his.

"There." He traces a finger down my arm and over my collarbone. He circles the lock that rests in the hollow of my throat. "You're mine."

Oh god, he needs to fuck me already. I spread my legs, and he groans at the sight of my wet pussy. "I need you inside me." The words spill out, desperate. "Please, Sebastian. I need to know what it means to be—"

He leans down and sucks a nipple into his mouth. The sensation shoots straight to my clit.

"Oh god—to be yours, please—"

He switches to the other nipple. My hips buck up, searching for friction that isn't there.

"Sebastian!"

"Patience." He kisses down my stomach and stops just above my pussy. "I get to decide what I want to give you, and when."

Oooh, god. His breath is warm against my pussy. I'm so wet I can feel it on my thighs.

"You're dripping." He sounds smug. "Is that for me?"

"It's for the collar." I'm gasping. "My pussy really liked the collar."

He laughs in surprise, and then his tongue is on me in one long lick from entrance to clit. I cry out, spine arching off the bed, and the collar presses against my throat as I gasp.

"Fuuuck."

"Mmm." He does it again, slower this time. "You taste like you're mine."

"I am," I gasp. "Yours!"

He circles my clit with his tongue with a light, teasing pressure. It's not enough.

"I could keep you here for hours." His fingers slide through my wetness, gathering it. "Edge you until you're crying and you beg me to let you come."

"I'm already begging." I pull against the restraints. "Please."

"What do you need?"

"Your cock." There's no dignity left. None. "I need you to fuck me and claim me. I'm yours."

He crawls up my body, settling between my thighs. The head of his cock brushes against my entrance.

Not in. Against.

"Say it again."

"I'm yours."

He presses forward. Just the tip. I whine.

"And?"

"And I need you to fuck me. Please. I need to feel you inside me, I need—"

He drives in. One long stroke that fills me completely.

I cry out in pleasure and rock against him.

"This pussy is mine." He pulls back and thrusts deep again. "Say it."

"Yours—pussy—yours."

"This body." Another thrust, this time harder. "Mine."

"Yes!"

"This heart." He stops moving, buried to the hilt, and his hand presses flat against my chest. Against my racing pulse. "This is mine too. Isn't it?"

My eyes are burning, and I'm suddenly struggling not to cry.

"Yes. All of it. Everything."

He fucks me slowly. "I'm going to make you come with my collar around your throat. Every time you touch that lock, you're going to remember this. Remember what it means to be claimed by me."

I whimper because I know he's right.

He pulls almost all the way out, then sinks back in while I moan. His hand traces the chain at my neck. "I want to watch this lock bounce against your throat while I fuck you."

He gets onto his knees and puts my feet on his shoulders. When he drives into me, the angle is deeper. Every thrust jolts me, and I can feel the collar bouncing.

"You're my good girl." He picks up the pace. "Wearing my collar while you come on my cock."

I'm close. Already so close. The pressure is building, coiling tight in my core, and the sound of him fucking me, wet and obscene, fills the room.

"Oooh, god, can I come? Please?"

"Come." He slams into me. "Now."

I cry out as pleasure ripples from my fingertips to my toes. Every nerve ending fires at once, and I clasp around him so hard it almost hurts. I close my eyes as waves of rapture sweep through my entire body.

"Perfect." His rhythm falters. "You're perfect. You're mine—"

He comes with a groan that vibrates through me. I feel the hot pulse of him flooding me as he presses me into the mattress. We're both gasping, trembling, wrecked.

When he finally softens and pulls out, he immediately unties my wrists and checks to make sure they're okay.

All I can do is curl into him and cry from the overwhelming weight of being so completely wanted. He holds me and strokes my hair, pressing kisses to my temple. He doesn't ask questions; he just lets me fall apart in his arms.

"I've got you." His voice is low against my hair. "I've always got you."

And deep down, I believe him.

Later, once we're cleaned up and back in bed, I touch the collar again. It's warm now and already feels like it's part of me.

It's going to be weird walking into work tomorrow wearing it hidden under my blouse, but also thrilling.

"I love this," I whisper to him.

"Yeah?"

I nod against his chest. "I don't know how to explain why."

"Try."

"It's like..." I search for the words. "You saw all my broken parts and didn't run. You locked them to you instead."

His arms tighten. "You never have to hide with me."

I press my face into his chest and breathe him in. "Sebastian?"

"Hmm?"

"Someday." My finger traces circles on his skin. "I want you to give me a ring. I want to wear both."

His breath catches.

"Both?"

I tilt my head up. "When we're ready, I want everything."

A few months ago, wanting everything would've sent me into a panic spiral. Wanting *anything* would've. Now I'm asking for it out loud.

And okay, I'm still a little terrified, but it's the good kind. The kind that means this matters.

The smile that breaks across his face makes my chest hurt.

"Someday," he promises. "You'll have everything."

He kisses me as if he's sealing the promise, and when I fall asleep in his arms, the weight of his collar against my throat feels like coming home.

Chapter 16

The Nelson presentation is in twenty minutes, and I'm going to die. My heart will give out somewhere around slide seven—the one with the org restructuring timeline—and they'll have to carry my body out of the conference room while Patricia Nelson watches with that legendary ice-queen expression everyone talks about.

I've run through these slides forty times. I could present them in my sleep, which is good because I barely slept last night. I stared at the ceiling and imagined every possible way this could go wrong.

Forty-two million dollars. Three hundred employees. A founder who's turned down two buyers already because she didn't trust their plans for her people.

No pressure.

The conference room fills with bodies. Twelve executives line the long table. Patricia Nelson sits at the opposite end, her silver-blonde hair immaculate, with reading glasses perched on her nose as she reviews the printed proposal I sent ahead. She hasn't looked up once.

Sebastian takes a seat in the back corner and crosses his arms. His face gives absolutely nothing away. He's in full CEO mode. No encouraging glances or subtle nods. I have to force myself not to touch the collar at my throat to steady myself.

"Ms. Hart." Patricia Nelson's voice cuts through the room. "Whenever you're ready."

When I speak, my voice doesn't shake, which is a minor miracle. "Thank you for the opportunity to present Ashford Holdings' integration strategy for Nelson Industries."

The first three slides are foundational, with the company overview and acquisition rationale. My voice sounds like it belongs to someone competent and calm, and not someone who is actively dying inside.

By slide four, Patricia Nelson takes off her reading glasses.

By slide seven—the org restructuring timeline—she's leaning forward.

"You're proposing parallel operations for the first year." She interrupts, tapping the printed page. "That's unusual. Most acquirers want immediate consolidation."

Here it is. The moment that either makes me or breaks me.

"Most acquirers tank productivity in the first eighteen months because they prioritize headcount savings." I click to my supporting data. "Your operations team runs at sixty percent efficiency on metrics that don't account for the specialized workflows they've developed over fifteen years. Our team runs on standardized systems. An immediate direct merge doesn't create synergy; it creates chaos."

Patricia's eyebrow rises, and I keep going.

"Parallel operations lets your team maintain their workflows while we facilitate gradual alignment. Your people learn our standards organically instead of making everyone rush to update their resume." There's a small ripple of laughter from the finance team. "We protect productivity and give your senior team a reason to stay instead of jumping ship to competitors who'll promise them the autonomy we just stripped away."

I click to the retention package slide. "Speaking of which—here's what we're offering your top thirty employees to ensure continuity through transition."

Patricia studies the numbers. The room is silent except for the soft hum of the projector.

"You built something worth protecting," I say, and I'm not performing anymore. I mean it. "The integration strategy should reflect that. Eighteen months to full operational merge. Your legacy intact, and your people taken care of."

For a long moment, Patricia Nelson doesn't speak, and then she looks at Sebastian. "Where did you find her?"

"She was with Mercer when we acquired them." His voice is neutral, but I catch the flicker of pride in his eyes. "We saw her potential immediately."

Patricia turns back to me and studies me with those sharp eyes that have reportedly made grown men cry in negotiations.

"This is exactly what I needed." She sets down the proposal. "I've turned down two buyers who treated my company like a spreadsheet. You're the first person who's treated it like something I built."

The relief hits so hard my knees almost buckle.

I did it.

The meeting wraps up with handshakes and next steps and Patricia Nelson telling me to call her Patricia. Sebastian hangs back while the room empties, and when it's just the two of us, his corporate mask finally falls.

"Well done." His eyes linger on my neck, where my collar is hidden. "Dinner tonight at my place. Seven o'clock." He brushes past me, close enough that I feel the heat of him. "Don't dress up."

He's out the door before I can ask what that means.

Tessa catches me in the hallway, grinning like she witnessed the whole thing through the glass walls.

"Patricia Nelson just called you 'exactly what we needed.' Do you understand how insane that is? She makes grown men cry. Actual tears."

"I think I blacked out for part of it."

"You were incredible." She squeezes my arm. "Seriously. That parallel ops angle? Daniel's been bragging about it to anyone who'll listen."

The validation settles in my chest. "Thanks, Tessa."

"Now go home and celebrate with your man." She winks. "You've earned it."

When I stop at my apartment to change, I try not to freak out.

I fail.

What if today was a test and I passed, but now he's going to tell me we need to slow down? What if Patricia Nelson changed her mind after I left? What if—

My phone buzzes.

Sebastian: Stop spiraling. I can feel it from here.

I text back.

Elise: I'm not spiraling. I'm mentally preparing.

Sebastian: Same thing. See you at 7.

He knows me too well. It's annoying. It's also the reason I love him.

Love.

God, I love him. I've been circling the thought for weeks, refusing to name it. Probably since the first time he held me through subdrop, and most definitely when he locked the collar around my throat and called it a promise.

I love him.

The thought terrifies me. Wanting things is how you get hurt. Loving people is how you get left.

But I'm tired of being afraid, and Sebastian is pretty damn amazing.

His apartment smells like garlic when I walk in. Takeout containers line the kitchen counter. It's not cheap takeout. It's from that Italian place with the six-week waitlist.

"You ordered from Vigilia's?" I set down my purse. "How?"

"I know people." He pulls me in for a kiss. "We needed to celebrate. You were incredible today. Nelson doesn't impress easily."

"I learned from the best."

"You learned from yourself." He hands me a plate already assembled with shrimp pasta, fresh parsley, the cream sauce I mentioned wanting to try a couple of weeks ago.

We eat at his kitchen island. Just two people and good pasta, talking about Nelson's legendary temper, and normal, everyday things.

It should feel easy, but the three words are lodged in my throat and bursting to get out.

After dinner, he pulls me onto the couch and wraps his arm around me. The city glitters through floor-to-ceiling windows, and I wish I could relax, but I'm vibrating out of my skin with everything I'm not saying.

"You're tense." His lips brush my ear. "What's wrong?"

"Nothing's wrong."

"Elise." He uses that stern tone that somehow makes me always want to obey whatever he says. "Don't lie to me."

My lungs constrict. This is it. The moment.

Is there a way to say "I love you" that has an escape hatch? A trapdoor I can fall through if he doesn't say it back? I can't think of anything that will soften the blow if he rejects me.

God. My brain is useless in a crisis.

"I need to tell you something."

He goes still. "Okay."

"I'm scared to say it." The admission comes out small. "Because once I say it, I can't unsay it. And if you don't—if it's not—"

My throat closes. Excellent timing, body. Very helpful.

"Hey." He turns me in his arms, tips my chin up so I can't hide. "Whatever it is, you can tell me."

I search his face for any sign that tells me I'm crazy and going to regret saying it first.

There isn't one.

My heart is slamming so hard he must be able to hear it. My palms are slick.

"I love you."

The words rush out, clumsy and terrified and completely graceless. I watch his face and brace for him to flinch.

His voice is soft. "Say it again."

"I love you." I say it clearly, and a smile transforms his face. I don't want to look away. "I'm in love with you. I don't know when it happened, but it did, and I can't pretend anymore that this is just—"

He kisses me.

His hands cradle my face, and he kisses me like I just offered him the entire world. Our tongues twirl together, and I'm about two seconds from trying to rip his clothes off when he groans.

"I love you too. God, Elise. I love you so fucking much."

Relief crashes through me in a wave so strong I laugh. "I thought maybe for you it was just a dom-sub thing."

He pulls away enough to meet my eyes. His expression is fierce. "I love your brain and your body and your smart mouth. I love that you challenge me. I love that you submit to me not because you're weak but because you're strong enough to choose it. I've been terrified to say it because I didn't want to scare you off."

"You were scared, too?"

"Fucking terrified." He grins. "I don't fall for people. I don't need anyone. And then I walked into that conference room, and I've needed you every second since. But I've been afraid to push you. You always seemed one step away from running."

He's not wrong, and I kiss him because it's easier to pour my feelings into the kiss.

"Take me to bed," I whisper. "Please. I need you."

He stands, pulling me with him, and I tug on his hand to stop him.

"I want—" The phrase catches in my throat. We've fucked. We've played. We've done things that would require a glossary for most people. But this is different. "I want to make love."

He gives me that glorious smile of his again. "Your wish is my command."

When we get into the bedroom, he undresses me slowly and kisses every inch of revealed skin. His hands map my body like he's learning me all over again with new information. When I'm bare except for his collar, he lays me on the bed and looks at me.

My instinct is to make a joke about being inspected, but the heat in his gaze makes every thought in my head evaporate.

"I love you," he says again. Like he can't stop.

"I love you too."

I reach for him, and he quickly strips and covers my body with his. His cock presses hard against my thigh, but he doesn't rush.

He kisses down my neck, pausing at the collar before moving to my breasts with soft kisses and gentle suction.

"Sebastian…" I arch into his touch, fingers threading through his hair.

He moves lower. "Let me take care of you."

He settles between my legs, and when his tongue slides through my folds, I gasp. He licks and sucks like he has all the time in the world. He doesn't stop, not even when I get close to coming. There's no denial tonight, just building pleasure in waves.

My body dissolves into a puddle of bliss.

"Please," I moan. "I want you inside me when I come."

He lifts his head, his chin shiny with my wetness, and grins at me. "That can be arranged."

He rises over me, positions himself at my entrance, and pauses.

"I love you," he says.

"I love you." My voice breaks on it.

He pushes inside, and we both gasp. The stretch is familiar, but the context changes everything. He makes love to me with long strokes, and every inch of him massages nerve endings I didn't even know I had. I wrap my legs around him and pull him deeper.

"You feel incredible." His forehead presses to mine. "Every time. But tonight—"

"I know." I moan as we rock together.

We find our rhythm. It's not fast or desperate, and our eyes stay locked together with every thrust. It feels like our souls are entwined.

My orgasm builds slowly, the pleasure coiling through my body.

"I'm close," I whisper.

"Me too." He groans. "Come with me."

The thought of us coming together does it. My whole body arches, clenching around him so hard I'm surprised he doesn't make a noise about it. Pleasure floods through me, and he follows seconds later, filling me with ropes of cum and groaning like he's surrendering.

We stay tangled together afterward as we come down.

"Holy shit," he manages eventually.

I laugh, boneless against the sheets. "Yeah."

"Move in with me."

My brain stalls. "What?"

He lifts his head to look at me. He's completely serious. "Move in with me. I'm tired of counting the nights until you're here. I want to fall asleep with you every night and wake up with you and make you coffee and—" He stops and laughs at himself. "Too much too fast. Forget I—"

"Yes."

His eyebrows shoot up. "Yes?"

"Yes." I sit up, matching his intensity. "I want that. All of that." My words tumble out.

He kisses me, and my heart sings with joy. It's a kiss full of promise.

"You can move in this weekend. Tomorrow. Right now, if you want." He pulls me against his chest. "Whatever you want."

His reaction makes me giggle, and I snuggle against him, wrapped in his arms and trying to process what happened. An hour ago, I was terrified to say I love you. Now I'm moving in with him. My life is shifting so fast I can barely track it.

But for once, the speed doesn't scare me. It feels right.

"Sebastian?"

"Mm?"

"I love you."

"I love you too." He tucks me closer. "More than I thought possible."

I fall asleep with his arms around me and his heartbeat under my ear.

CHAPTER 17

Two weeks later, Sebastian's hand finds my hip before I'm fully awake. It's not a sexual touch, it's just a gentle pressure. I press back against him, and his arm tightens, pulling me closer. "Morning." His voice is rough with sleep.

"Mmm." I twist to face him. He looks softer in the early light. "What day is it?"

"Sunday."

Sunday. The word takes a moment to sink in. "What time?"

"Early enough." He traces my collarbone, fingertip following the chain to where the lock rests. "We have brunch with Eleanor at eleven."

That cuts through the sleepy fog. "Brunch?"

"My mother. Remember?"

Right. Eleanor. The woman who helped shape him into the man I get to keep.

Today I'll meet her.

My stomach performs a complicated acrobatic routine. Anxiety upgraded to full production value—costumes, choreography, the works.

"Stop worrying." He kisses my forehead and pulls me closer. We stay like that for a while, tangled together, not talking. This is the kind of quiet I didn't know existed before him.

I moved in a week ago, and I'm finally all unpacked. That still doesn't help me figure out what to wear today to meet his mother. I'm standing in front of our closet in my third outfit, seriously considering faking my own death.

What does one wear to meet the mother of the man whose collar you wear around your throat? I should have escaped to Canada to become that sheep farmer. Sheep don't care about what you're wearing or give a shit about making good first impressions.

The first outfit was too formal, like I was interviewing for the position of Acceptable Girlfriend™.

The second was too casual. Jeans and a sweater that screamed I don't care what you think of me, which was a lie so transparent even the sweater seemed embarrassed.

This third one—a simple wrap dress in deep green—might work. Sophisticated but not uptight. Feminine without being a try-hard.

My hands shake as I fasten small gold earrings. I survived Lydia Kessler's targeted campaign to destroy my career. I've knelt naked for a man who could dismantle me with a single word. Why does meeting his mother terrify me more than any of that?

Because mothers see through you. That's their whole deal. And if Eleanor looks at me and sees what everyone else has always seen—forgettable, too much effort, not worth the hassle of keeping—

"You've been staring at the mirror for ten minutes."

I jump at his words. Sebastian fills the doorway, already dressed, watching me with an expression I can't decode.

"I'm mentally preparing."

"For brunch?"

"For judgment." I smooth the dress over my hips. "What if she hates me?"

"She won't hate you."

"What if she thinks I'm not good enough for you?"

He crosses to me and turns me away from the mirror. "She's going to love you. Because I love you. And because you're exactly the kind of woman who deserves to be loved—even if you don't believe it yet."

"That's very romantic." My voice cracks. "But I'm still terrified."

"I know." He kisses my forehead. "You look beautiful. Let's go."

Eleanor Ashford is nothing like I expected.

I'd built her in my head as someone severe and polished. The kind of woman who raises a man like Sebastian would be controlled and commanding. Probably terrifying.

The woman who opens the door of her brownstone wears paint-stained jeans and a smile that crinkles the corners of her eyes.

"You must be Elise." She pulls me into a hug before I can extend my hand.

She hugs like it's easy. Like people just...do this.

My arms lift awkwardly, and I pat her shoulder like she's a coworker I'm congratulating on a mediocre quarterly report. Very smooth.

Definitely not the behavior of someone who wants to give the best impression.

She pulls back and studies my face for a beat too long. Whatever she's looking for, she must find it, because her smile softens. "He was right. You have kind eyes."

"Mother." Sebastian's voice carries a warning, but he's smiling.

"What? I've been waiting weeks to meet her." She shoots Sebastian a look that's probably been making him squirm since he was twelve. "He's been keeping you to himself."

"Can you blame me?" He pulls me against his side. "I don't like to share."

Eleanor's brownstone is the opposite of Sebastian's sleek minimalism. Art crowds every wall. Books stack on every surface in precarious towers. Plants fight for window space like they're competing for attention.

It smells like turpentine and baking bread. It smells like someone messy and creative lives here.

"You're an artist," I say, studying a half-finished canvas propped against the dining room wall.

"Retired art teacher. Now I paint for myself." She waves us toward the kitchen. "Come, come. I made quiche."

Over brunch, Eleanor fills in the pieces Sebastian didn't give me. "He told you about the weeks of silence?"

I nod, glancing at Sebastian. He's watching his mother with a happy expression.

"What he didn't tell you"—Eleanor refills my wine without asking—"is that I was terrified."

"Terrified?"

"He was my fourth foster placement in three years. The other three went back into the system within months." She sets down the bottle, and her hands aren't quite steady. "I kept failing and kept thinking I wasn't cut out for this."

Sebastian goes very still beside me.

"And then this kid shows up with a chip on his shoulder the size of Manhattan, and he won't look at me, won't speak, just sits in the corner reading, like if he ignores me long enough, I'll leave him alone." She laughs, but there's a rawness underneath it. "I almost gave up. The third week, I called the caseworker to request a transfer."

"You never told me that." Sebastian's voice is soft.

"Because I didn't go through with it." Eleanor reaches across the table and squeezes his hand. "I hung up the phone and made you a grilled cheese sandwich instead. Sat outside your door and ate mine while you ate yours on the other side. I didn't say a word. Just sat there."

My throat is closing. I'm thinking about doors and grilled cheese and all the ways people show up for each other without saying anything at all.

"The next day, you came downstairs for breakfast." Eleanor's eyes are bright. "First time in three weeks. You didn't talk. Just sat at the table and waited for me to make eggs."

"I remember," Sebastian says quietly. "You made them scrambled. I hate scrambled."

"I know. You told me eventually." She wipes her eyes. "It took you another month to use actual words, but you told me."

The family we choose. That's what this is. What Sebastian built with his team—Tessa, Daniel, Cora. What he learned here, in this kitchen that smells like bread and turpentine. From a woman who almost gave up but made a grilled cheese sandwich instead.

After brunch, Eleanor shows me her studio, a converted sunroom drowning in canvases and the chaos of creation. Sebastian hangs in the doorway, watching us like he's not sure whether to intervene.

"He's different with you," Eleanor says quietly, sorting through tubes of paint. "Softer. More himself."

"He's the first person who made me think I was allowed to want things."

She turns to face me, and her expression is knowing in a way that makes me wonder exactly how much Sebastian has told her. "He spent thirty years convinced he was too intense to be loved," Eleanor says. "Too demanding. That anyone who got close would eventually leave." She glances at her son in the doorway, then turns her gaze back to me. "You stayed."

"I chose to stay." My fingers find the collar at my throat—a gesture that's become instinct. "And I'd choose it again. Every time."

Eleanor's eyes flick to the collar—a single heartbeat—and her smile deepens. "Good. That's all I needed to know."

On the drive home, Sebastian's hand finds mine across the console.

"She approved of you," he says. "In case that wasn't clear."

"She seemed to."

"She told me while you were in the bathroom. She said I should marry you before you come to your senses."

My heart pounds. "She said that?"

"She also said to tell you she's planning to teach you to paint. Whether you want to learn or not." He squeezes my hand. "Fair warning."

"I can't paint."

"Neither could I. She doesn't care."

I let the warmth spread through me. Eleanor. The team at work. Sebastian's hand in mine. "I love you."

He pulls my hand to his lips. "I love you too."

CHAPTER 18

A month into living with him. My books crowd his shelves. And apparently, my curiosity has zero boundaries and no shame. I've decided it's time for a change of pace tonight.

Sebastian is in a meeting downtown and won't be home for a couple hours. I told myself I'd do a little work on our next merger while I waited for him, but instead, I'm rifling through his collection of sex toys like a perverted archaeologist. For science. Very important, horny science.

I find what I'm looking for in the drawer of the playroom cabinet. The nipple clamps are silver and connected by a delicate chain. They almost look like elegant jewelry, but they should probably come with a warning label and possibly a waiver. My thumb runs over one of the adjustable screws, and my nipples tighten like they're already volunteering for duty. My body clearly doesn't care about the potential discomfort.

I've been curious about the clamps ever since I saw them. Now I just have to plot how to demand he use them on me.

He comes home around seven, loosening his tie as he walks through the door. I'm on the couch, pretending to read. The clamps are hidden under the throw pillow behind me like contraband.

"Long day?" I ask casually. Not at all sitting on top of evidence of my scheming.

"Endless." He tosses his jacket over a chair and drops beside me. His hand finds my thigh automatically. "Henley's lawyers are playing games. We'll close anyway, but it's tedious."

"Poor baby." I press a kiss to his jaw. "Want me to help you unwind?"

"Always." His fingers dig into my thigh, and heat pools low in my belly. "What did you have in mind?"

Okay. Here goes. It's time to be a sexually empowered woman and take what I want. I reach behind the cushion and pull out the clamps.

His eyebrows rise. "Someone was exploring the playroom."

I dangle them by the chain, watching the silver catch the light. "You said they require trust. I trust you. And I want to try them."

His expression shifts to that hungry focus that means I've surprised and pleased him. "You're sure?"

"I'm sure." I set the clamps in his palm, curl his fingers around them. My whole body is vibrating. "But I have conditions."

"Conditions." He smiles. "What are my submissive's conditions?"

The way he says that makes me question my plan. Can submissives make demands? Is this allowed? Is there a committee I should have petitioned?

"Your submissive has been thinking about this all afternoon." I straddle his lap, facing him. His cock stiffens beneath me, which I'm taking as a vote of confidence from the relevant committee. "I want to try them. But I want to be in control of when they come off. I want to set the pace."

He's quiet for a moment, studying my face.

My brain offers helpful contributions like *he's going to say no* and *you've ruined the dynamic* and *this is why you can't have nice things.*

"You want to top from the bottom," he says finally.

I'm not really sure what that means, but I go with it. "I want to *choose* my own intensity." I take his face in my hands. "I trust you completely, and I want the pain, but I want to ride you while I decide how much."

I'm not sure I'm making sense, so I try again. "I want to take what I want instead of waiting for permission to want it."

"You want to show me you're not passive and you're choosing this." His voice has gone rough, and my clit throbs in response.

"Yes." I rock my hips, grinding against his cock. My pussy has officially taken over negotiations, and she is not known for her restraint. "So here's what's going to happen. You're going to sit there and let me undress. Then I'm going to tell you exactly how tight to make them. And then I'm going to ride you. I'll decide when they come off. Understood?"

The groan he makes is half surrender, half desire. "Understood."

I stand up and take my time peeling off my shirt slowly. I let him watch as I unclasp my bra and slide it down my arms. My nipples are already stiff in anticipation, and also, let's be honest, the absolute power trip of having Sebastian sitting on the couch waiting for *my* instructions.

This is what it feels like to take what I want. The control freak who lives in my chest is losing her mind in the best way. She's updating her resume to include "Successfully Dominated a Dominant" under skills.

"Touch my nipples," I instruct. "Get them ready."

He rolls my nipples between his fingers gently, then harder, pinching until I gasp. Pleasure shoots straight to my clit. I'm already wet and aching.

"Harder."

He obeys. The pinch sharpens, riding that edge where pleasure meets pain, and I moan. My hands find his shoulders for balance as sparks light up my nervous system.

"Now." I reach for the clamps. "Put the first one on."

He takes it from me, slides it over my nipple, and adjusts the screw. "This tight?"

Ooooh fuck. Wow, um, that's sharp.

"That's good." I try to keep my voice calm. "Now the other."

He positions it over my left nipple, and I watch his face as he releases the clamp.

The bite is *exquisite.* A hiss escapes me as the pain fades into a throbbing pulse that seems connected directly to my pussy. Every heartbeat sends a wave from my nipple down.

"Color?" His voice is strained.

"Oh no, you don't," I laugh, breathless. "I'm in control, remember?"

The dual sensation on my nipples makes me dizzy. It's a constant, inescapable awareness of my nipples. The chain swings gently between them.

Looking down, I admire the clamps. I chose this and demanded it. My nipples throb, and I suddenly need his cock inside me.

"Get your cock out," I order. "Now."

He strips while I shimmy out of my leggings. When I straddle him again, I sink down onto his cock, and we both groan.

"Fuck, you feel good." He grasps my hips as I rock against him.

The stretch is familiar, but the clamps add another layer. Movement makes the chain sway and tug the clamps. It's a circuit of pleasure connecting everything–his cock, my pussy, the clamps, the bite.

I ride him, enjoying being in control for a change.

"Fuck," he breathes. "You're so—"

"Shh." I press a finger to his lips. "Don't talk. Just feel."

His jaw tightens, but he obeys. His hands stay on my hips, steadying without guiding. Letting me set the pace.

I roll my hips slowly, savoring the drag of his cock inside me. The chain swings with each motion, tugging, sending sparks until the pleasure and pain blur together.

"Tug the chain," I gasp.

His finger hooks through it and pulls gently.

I almost scream.

"Again. Harder."

He pulls, and the clamps tighten, and I shatter around him without warning—an orgasm that rips through me with no buildup. I bounce on his cock, milking him, as I cry out in ecstasy.

"Don't come," I manage, still shaking. "Not yet. I'm not done."

He groans, but he obeys.

Good boy.

I don't say it out loud. But I think it.

I ride him through the aftershocks of pleasure, slower now, drawing out each wave. The clamps throb in time with my heartbeat. Every nerve is exposed, oversensitive, too much and not enough at the same time.

"Elise—"

"What did I say about talking?"

He groans, head falling back against the couch. His cock pulses inside me, desperate, denied.

And I love it. I love having him at my mercy for once, this man who controls everything, reduced to sounds and straining muscles and the desperate need to come. His jaw is clenched tight, and I can see the muscle jumping. His cock is so hard inside me it's practically vibrating with the effort of not coming.

I pick up the pace. Fuck myself on him harder, faster, chasing another peak while he watches with wild eyes. The chain bounces against my chest. The clamps send jolts that blur pleasure into pain until the distinction stops mattering.

"I'm going to take one off now," I tell him.

I reach up and release the left clamp.

The sensation is *blinding*. Fire and ice and pins and needles, shooting from my nipple through my entire body. I cry out, clenching around his cock so hard he groans.

"Fuck fuck fuck—"

"Keep riding." His voice is wrecked. "Don't stop."

I don't. Can't. I'm grinding against him, oblivious to anything but the pleasure. When I release the second clamp, the rush of blood sends me screaming into another orgasm—harder than the first, my whole body seizing around him in ecstasy.

"Come," I gasp. "Now. Fill me up."

He erupts with a growl. His hips surge upward as jets of warm cum fill me. I can feel every twitch of his cock, every spurt of cum as I ride him until he's completely spent.

We collapse together. Breathing hard. My nipples throb, tender and sensitive, and I can't stop smiling.

"Holy shit." His voice is hoarse. "What the hell was that?"

"That was me." I kiss his jaw, his cheek, the corner of his mouth. "Sometimes I choose to take what I want."

He's quiet for a moment before wrapping his arms around me and toppling us over to snuggle on the couch.

"You terrify me sometimes," he murmurs. "In the best way."

"Good." I settle into his arms with him as the big spoon. "That's how you make me too. Terrified and safe."

He strokes my side, and I'm pleasantly boneless. After a few minutes, he extracts himself, and I whimper as he gets up.

"Stay there."

He disappears toward the kitchen, and I take stock of my body. My nipples are tender enough that even the brush of air makes me shiver. But it's a good kind of sore.

He comes out of the kitchen with two bowls.

"Is that..." I squint. "Ice cream?"

"Mint chip." He hands me a bowl.

"Sebastian Ashford, CEO of Ashford Acquisitions, is feeding me ice cream while his cum drips down my thigh." I take a bite. "This is not the aftercare protocol I expected."

"Would you prefer champagne and strawberries?"

"God, no." I shovel another spoonful into my mouth. Mmm, it's really good. "This is perfect."

He settles next to me, his own bowl balanced on his knee. He's still naked and gorgeous.

"I liked it," he says finally. "Being told what to do there."

"You did?"

"I didn't expect to." He frowns at his ice cream. "Control is...it's what I do. What I'm good at. But giving it to you—" He grins at me. "You could do that again occasionally."

My heart does a flip-twist-squeeze combination. Yeah, I love this man. "I suppose I could ride you again at some point."

"Just don't expect me to give up control every time." His voice shifts, and there's the dom again, lurking beneath the post-sex softness. "Next time, I'm putting those clamps on you myself. And I'm deciding when they come off."

Desire flares low in my belly. Even now, even after two orgasms, my body responds to his authority.

"Promise?"

"Count on it."

I smile around my spoon and lean into his side.

Eating ice cream naked with a man who lets me boss him around and promises to put me in my place is the strangest, best thing that's ever happened to me.

The fear this will all vanish is still there, and maybe it always will be. But it's quieter tonight. It's drowned out by mint chip and tender nipples and the steady warmth of him beside me.

Tonight, I'll let myself have this.

CHAPTER 19

The pill pack sits in my palm. The row of tiny white pills are mocking me.

I've been staring at it for seven minutes. Seven minutes of my life devoted to a hormone tablet the size of a Tic Tac. It's been the same routine every morning: wake up, reach for the nightstand, swallow on autopilot.

Today, my brain has decided to stage a rebellion because I keep thinking about Sebastian's hand pressed flat against my belly after he fills me with cum and murmuring *someday* like it was a prayer.

What if someday is now?

My thumb traces the edge of the blister pack. One little hormone tablet standing between fantasy and reality. Between dirty talk and actually trying. Between "I want to breed you," whispered hot against my neck, and *oh shit, we might actually make a human being.*

The jury—still my pussy—has already voted. She's not known for her patience or her risk assessment skills. She's been sending memos for weeks. The memos say YES in all caps with several exclamation points and a confetti emoji.

But my brain won't shut up. What if I'm not ready?

I'm twenty-six. I was eating cereal for dinner just weeks ago, standing over the sink like a raccoon in a cardigan. What if I ruin a child the way I was ruined?

I don't remember my mother, but I remember the shape of her absence, the way it settled into every corner of every foster home, every temporary bedroom, every "we're so sorry, sweetie, but this placement isn't working out." What if I pass that on? What if abandonment is genetic, and I leave the way she left?

What if I finally have the one thing I've always wanted, and then I lose it?

Everyone leaves eventually. That's the lesson, right? The curriculum of my entire childhood. Don't want things. Wanting things is how you get hurt.

Except I do want this.

God, I want this so much my chest aches with it.

Every time Sebastian comes inside me and I feel his cum, every time he whispers about filling me up, breeding me, making me round with his baby, my whole body lights up. Like every cell got the memo. Like I was built for exactly this moment, to want exactly this thing, and I've been fighting it with logic and fear and a tiny white pill.

I set the pill pack down and close the lid.

Holy shit. Did I really do that?

My hands are shaking. But there's this weird calm underneath the panic. This certainty that has no business existing in my anxiety-riddled brain.

I want to try. For real. Not someday. Now.

He finds me on the balcony after work. I'm bundled in a blanket like a melancholy burrito, watching rush hour crawl along the streets below. The city doesn't care that my entire life might be about to change.

"You okay?" Sebastian hands me a glass of wine, drops into the chair beside me. "Work getting to you?"

"No, that went fine." I take a sip. Let the warmth settle. "I've been thinking."

"About?"

Here goes everything.

"About what I want." I turn to face him, and his eyes sharpen with laser focus that means I have his complete undivided attention. "About a baby."

His jaw tightens. "A baby?"

"Yeah." My heart is doing its best hummingbird impression. "I didn't take my pill this morning."

The words hang there, and his breath catches.

"You said we'd wait until I was ready and knew in my bones this was permanent." I set down my wine because my hands are shaking. "I'm ready. I want to actually try. Not someday. Now." I reach for his hand because I need to touch him. "I want you to put a baby in me."

The words send heat flooding through my core. This isn't just dirty talk anymore.

"I want you to fill me up and give me everything."

He groans, and his hands shake as he pulls me against him. "You're sure?"

"I'm sure." I squeeze his hand. "I love you. I want to have your baby. It's all I think about."

"All you think about?"

"When you come inside me." I hold his gaze. No point being shy about it now. "Every single time. I think about it being real."

He takes my face in his hands. "I think about it too." His voice cracks. "Every time. Wondering if this will be the one. Knowing it won't be, but wanting it anyway."

"Then let's do it."

He kisses me softly, and then he's lifting me out of the chair. I yelp because I'm still in my burrito blanket.

"Sebastian!"

"You told me you want to have my baby." He's carrying me inside. "We're starting now."

I laugh at him. "The pill isn't out of my system, you goof."

"Don't care." He sets me down in the bedroom and removes the blanket.

Suddenly, I'm desperate for him. I yank his shirt over his head. "I want to know what it's like when it's real. When you're not holding back."

He strips off the rest of his clothes and then mine. When we're on the bed, he settles between my thighs. His cock is hard against my hip, already slick at the tip.

"If this works—" His voice is rough. "If you get pregnant—"

"Then I get pregnant." I pull him down and kiss him deeply. "That's the point, genius."

He pushes inside me slowly. Nothing between us but want and hope and the terrifying possibility of creating a tiny human.

"God." He bottoms out and grinds against me. "I've wanted this so long." His voice breaks on the words. "I've wanted to breed you for real. Not dirty talk. Actually give you my baby."

"Then do it." I clench around him. "Stop holding back. Take what's yours."

His control snaps. He fucks me hard and fast, driving so deep I can feel every drag of his cock.

"Mine," he snarls against my throat. "This pussy is mine."

"Yours!"

"Going to fill you up." His pace is relentless. "Going to come so deep inside you."

"Please—" I'm already close. "Please, I want it, I want to feel you."

He reaches between us and rubs my clit in that perfect rhythm he's learned over the weeks. When I explode, I practically levitate off the bed. I'm convulsing and moaning as pleasure shoots through every inch of my body.

He slams deep and shudders as he erupts. He keeps fucking me as he unloads every single drop deep inside, filling me up with everything he has.

When he finally stills, we're both shaking.

"We might have made a baby," he says. Wonderstruck.

"We might have." I stroke his hair, kiss his temple. "But we probably will have to keep trying. Oh no. What a hardship."

He laughs, and we lie tangled together as his cum leaks out of me. I float in my happy place and let myself believe this might actually work.

Three weeks later.

Sebastian has been acting weird all week. He's checking his phone constantly and disappearing for hushed conversations with the team. He's coming home with shopping bags he shoves into closets before I can see the logos.

My period is three days late. I haven't told him. Haven't taken a test. Haven't even bought one because that would require confirming whether I'm pregnant or just late, and I'm not sure which answer scares me more.

"Wear something nice tonight." He says it over breakfast, wearing that controlled expression that means he's planning something. "I'm taking you out."

"Where?"

"It's a surprise."

Suspicion prickles down my spine. I guess I finally get to figure out what he's up to. Either he's proposing or I've wandered into a very elaborate practical joke. Given our history, I'm putting my money on option one. My stomach does a complicated flip that might be excitement or terror or both.

Later that night, Sebastian doesn't come home, but he tells me a car will come and pick me up. I choose my favorite green dress that I rarely have a reason to wear, and I'm vacillating between excitement and freaking out when the car arrives.

It's not his usual town car. It's a stretch limo with fairy lights and champagne and a single red rose on the seat.

So. Definitely not a joke.

The limo stops at the waterfront. White lights drip from every surface of a yacht so gorgeous it belongs in a magazine. Sebastian stands at the gangway in a charcoal suit, looking at me with love.

We take an evening cruise on the yacht, and there's dinner below deck. The food is delicious and his hand keeps finding mine across the table. But underneath it all, anticipation hums through my bloodstream like electricity.

After dessert, he leads me to the front of the yacht. The wind whips my hair into chaos.

He wraps his jacket around my shoulders and turns me to face him.

"I had a speech prepared." His voice is rough. "Pages of it. Everything I wanted to say about how you changed my life."

"Oh, Sebastian."

"But I'm not going to give you the speech." He reaches into his pocket. "Because the truth is simpler than anything I could write."

He drops to one knee, and my heart stops. The world narrows to this single moment: the yacht rocking beneath us, the city glittering behind him, this man on his knees looking up at me with complete love.

He's holding a velvet box, and his hands are shaking.

Sebastian Ashford's hands are shaking.

"I love you." His voice cracks, and the sound cracks me open with it. "I love who you are. I love who you're becoming. I love your strength and your submission and the way you make me want to be better."

He opens the box.

The ring catches the light and steals my breath. It's a princess-cut diamond, perfectly clear, set in a white gold band with smaller stones along the sides. It's beautiful and exactly what I would have chosen. The kind of ring that says *I know you* instead of *look what I can afford*.

My eyes are leaking before I register the tears.

"Marry me, Elise." His voice breaks on my name. "Be my wife. Let me spend forever earning what you've already given me."

"Yes."

"Yes?" He says it like he can't quite believe it. Like he needs to hear it again to make it real.

"Yes." My voice is steadier now, even though my whole body is trembling. "Obviously yes. Are you insane? Yes."

His face transforms. I've seen Sebastian Ashford in boardrooms, demolishing opponents with a single sentence. I've seen him in the playroom, commanding and in control. I've seen him after sex, soft and warm and impossibly tender.

I've never seen him like this. Relief floods his face—like he actually thought I might say no—then joy breaks through, and his eyes go bright with tears he doesn't try to hide.

His hands are shaking as he slides the ring onto my also-shaking finger. We're both vibrating from emotion.

It fits perfectly. Of course it does. Because he plans everything, and he probably borrowed one of my rings to get measured while I didn't even notice it was missing.

The weight of it settles against my skin. Mine.

I hold my hand up between us, watching the diamond catch the light from a thousand fairy lights strung across the yacht. My hand in front of the Manhattan skyline, wearing proof that someone is choosing to keep me forever.

"My fiancée." He says it as if he's testing the word.

"My future husband."

He pulls me against him and kisses me deeply. I tried not to think too much about how he'd propose, if he ever did, but this was more than I ever would have dreamed.

When we finally break apart, we're both crying and laughing at the same time.

"The ring is perfect," I manage. "How did you know?"

"I pay attention." His thumb traces circles on my palm, right next to where the diamond sits.

"You planned this whole thing." I gesture at the yacht, the lights, the city spread out behind us like a gift. "The limo. The dinner. All of it."

"I wanted it to be perfect."

"It is." I grab his face and kiss him again. "It's perfect. You're perfect. I can't believe you were nervous."

"You're the only thing in my life that makes me nervous." He tucks a strand of windswept hair behind my ear. "The only thing I can't afford to lose."

My throat tightens. After twenty-six years of being forgettable, of being easy to leave, this man is telling me I'm the thing he can't afford to lose.

"You won't lose me," I whisper. "I'm not going anywhere."

He presses his forehead to mine. "Promise?"

"Promise."

We stand there wrapped around each other while the yacht rocks beneath us. His hand finds my belly. Presses flat.

"Have you tested yet?"

I shake my head. "I'm late. I was scared."

"We'll test tomorrow." He kisses my forehead. "Together. Whatever the answer is."

"And if it's positive?"

His smile is blinding. "Then I get to marry you while you're carrying my baby."

I lean into him and wonder how I got so damn lucky.

The test takes three minutes.

One hundred eighty seconds. Three minutes should be nothing.

It's not nothing.

We sit on the edge of the bathtub together, the plastic stick on the counter. Sebastian's hand grips mine so tight I can feel his pulse hammering against my fingers. Or maybe that's mine. Hard to tell where he ends and I begin right now.

"This is worse than the Nelson presentation," I whisper.

He laughs, short and nervous. "Significantly higher stakes."

The timer on his phone hasn't chimed yet. It's been maybe forty-five seconds. Possibly forty-five years.

What if it's negative?

Disappointment. Crushing, stupid disappointment, even though we've only been trying for a few weeks. I know better than to expect instant results. But I'll still feel like I failed. Like my body—which has already failed me in so many ways, betrayed me so many times—has found one more way to let me down.

And having to keep trying isn't the worst problem. The trying part is excellent. Five stars. Would recommend.

But what if it takes months? What if it takes years? What if we're one of those couples who spends a fortune on fertility treatments and it still doesn't work and—

Shit, what if it's positive?

Terror. Pure, undiluted terror. I don't even want to think about everything that could go wrong.

"Hey." Sebastian's voice cuts through the spiral. His free hand finds my chin, tilts my face toward his. "Where'd you go?"

"Nowhere good." My laugh comes out watery. "The usual places."

"Tell me."

"I'm just scared."

"I know." He presses his forehead to mine. "I'm scared too. I spent thirty-eight years building walls. Then you knocked them all down, and now we're talking about creating someone who will have complete power to destroy me just by existing. Yeah. I'm scared."

"That's not comforting."

"It's not supposed to be." He kisses my nose. "It's supposed to be honest. We're both scared. We're doing it anyway. That's what bravery is."

The timer goes off, and neither of us moves.

The test is ready. The answer exists. Schrödinger's pregnancy has collapsed into one reality or the other, and all we have to do is look.

Stand up, I tell my legs. *Walk to the counter. Look at the test.*

My legs send back a polite decline. They're busy. Prior commitments. They've suddenly remembered they need to be literally anywhere else.

"Let's do this together," he says.

Okay, we're being dumb. I grab his hand and stand.

We cross to the counter.

Two lines.

Positive.

I stare at those two pink lines and my brain shorts out. Completely offline. No clever commentary. No self-deprecating jokes. Nothing but this impossible reality staring up at me from a piece of plastic.

Sebastian drops to his knees right there on the bathroom floor. His forehead presses against my belly, and his shoulders shake.

"Sebastian?"

"Give me a minute." His voice is absolutely destroyed. "I need a minute."

I sink my fingers into his hair, holding him against me while he processes. My own eyes burn.

The breeding kink that started as dirty talk and escalated into something we actually planned for, it's real now. Growing inside me. Already dividing cells or whatever babies do when they're the size of a poppy seed.

Holy shit. There's a tiny human in there because my egg and Sebastian's sperm had a very productive meeting.

"Hey." I tug gently, urging him to look up. His eyes are wet. "We did it."

"You did it." He presses a kiss to my stomach. "You're doing it. I contributed."

"Contributed." A wet laugh escapes me. "That's one word for it."

He stands and pulls me into his arms, holding me until I can barely breathe. "I love you. I love you so fucking much."

"I know." I bury my face in his chest. "And I love you too."

We stay like that. Holding each other and letting it sink in.

A baby. A ring. A future I never let myself want until he made it safe to reach for.

I keep waiting for the catch. For someone to jump out and yell *gotcha*. For the universe to remember it gave something to Elise Hart and demand it back with interest.

The catch doesn't come.

"Sebastian?"

"Mm?"

"I think I'm going to need more than three minutes to process this."

He laughs and kisses the top of my head. "Take all the time you need." His hand settles over my belly. "We have the rest of our lives."

The rest of our lives.

I'm standing in a bathroom with a ring on my finger, a baby in my belly, and a man who chose me. Who keeps choosing me. And I have zero desire to run.

I finally found the man who makes me want to stay.

EPILOGUE

"Stop fussing." I swat Tessa's hands away from the ribbon on the gift. "It's fine."

"It's crooked." She adjusts it anyway, then steps back. "There. Perfect."

The nursery is almost finished with its pale yellow walls, white furniture, a mobile of silver stars. Sebastian insisted on hiring decorators, but I wanted to do most of it myself. I wanted to touch every piece and arrange every corner to make it ours.

A year ago, it was easier to be invisible than to want things I couldn't have.

Now I'm decorating a nursery while a woman who voluntarily became my best friend fusses over ribbon placement like it's a matter of national security.

The bump is undeniable now. It's round and firm beneath my dress. I catch myself touching it constantly, this instinct to protect what's mine. My body did this. Is doing this. For once, she and I are on the same team.

We don't know if it's a girl or a boy. We chose not to know. But we have a bet going. I think it's a girl, and he thinks it's a boy. The winner has to do the midnight feedings for the first three months.

"You're glowing," Tessa says.

"I'm exhausted." I gesture at my swollen feet. "These ankles have given up on life. They've submitted their resignation. They're done. I pee every twenty minutes. And I cried yesterday because we ran out of pickles."

"Glowing," she repeats firmly. "Trust me."

The doorbell rings, and then there are voices in the hallway. Daniel's laugh, Cora's excited shriek, Eleanor's warm murmur underneath. Another male voice that I recognize as Tessa's husband, Seth.

They're all here for the shower. A room full of people who showed up for me.

My chest does that thing where it feels too full and too tight at the same time. Where I want to run and stay in equal measure. Where I don't know if I'm going to cry or laugh or possibly vomit because apparently pregnancy makes all three equally likely.

Who knew getting acquired by a hot billionaire would come with a built-in family? Best corporate merger ever.

"Ready?" Tessa squeezes my hand.

No. Yes. Maybe. My heart is pounding and my palms are sweating and the baby is kicking like she wants to be part of this, too.

"Ready."

The living room is chaos in the best way.

Daniel and Seth are arguing about stroller brands. Cora is making Eleanor try an app that predicts what the baby will look like.

"She has your nose and Sebastian's frown," Cora announces. "Very cute."

Sebastian stands by the window, watching it all with that expression I've learned means he's grateful and trying not to show how much this means to him.

He's failing. Everyone can tell. Nobody's pointing it out because we all have an unspoken agreement to pretend CEOs are emotionless robots.

I cross to him and slide under his arm. "You okay?"

"More than okay." He pulls me close, hand settling on the bump. "I keep thinking about what my life looked like a year ago in this empty condo. Work. Nothing else." His voice drops. "And now this." He kisses my temple. "You gave me everything."

"Pretty sure you gave me a few things too." I pat my belly. "Literally. With enthusiasm. Repeatedly."

"You're the one who begged."

I glance around to make sure no one is listening to us. Everyone is laughing and talking together.

"Sir, I'm carrying your enthusiastic contribution inside my body. She's pressing on my bladder like it owes her money."

He laughs, and the sound draws everyone's attention. Cora immediately starts snapping photos. Daniel raises his glass.

"To Elise and Sebastian," he announces. "Who somehow managed to be even more disgustingly in love than the rest of us."

"To the baby!" Cora adds. "Who's going to be spoiled rotten by every single person in this room."

"To family," Eleanor says quietly. "The kind we're born into, and the kind we build."

I look around the room at the people who became my family when I wasn't paying attention. At the ring on my finger. At the collar against my throat that nobody here finds strange. At the man whose hand rests protectively over our child.

A year ago, I was convinced I didn't deserve to want things.

Now I have everything.

And yeah, I still wake up at 3 a.m. sometimes, heart pounding, convinced it's all going to disappear. But then Sebastian's arm tightens around me in his sleep, and the baby kicks, and I remember I'm loved.

* * *

Three months later.

The delivery room is chaos. I'm screaming profanity, and Sebastian is pale but refusing to let go of my hand.

"One more push," the nurse says.

"You said that three pushes ago!" I yell. "You're a LIAR!"

Sebastian squeezes my hand. "You've got this."

"I hate your very effective reproductive system—"

One more push and then crying.

Not mine. Well, also mine. But also tiny, furious, unmistakably alive crying.

"It's a girl," someone says.

HA.

I win.

Midnight feedings are his problem.

That's the first thing I think. I'm not proud of it. I am who I am.

They place her on my chest, this squirming, red-faced, absolutely pissed-off miracle, and everything else disappears.

There's only her.

Only us.

Only this moment that splits my life into before and after.

We already had names chosen. "Haven," I whisper. "Hi, baby. Hi, Haven."

She's perfect. She's ours. She's screaming like she's personally offended by the concept of being born, which honestly? Fair. She was cozy in there.

Sebastian leans over us, tears streaming down his face. He looks at me like I've handed him the universe wrapped in a tiny blanket.

Which, I kind of did. She weighs seven pounds. The universe has never been so small or so heavy.

"Haven Eleanor," he says, voice breaking. "She's here."

I'm exhausted and exhilarated and so in love it's absurd. "She's here."

He kisses my forehead, my cheek, the corner of my mouth. "You're stuck with me now."

"Promise?"

"Forever."

Haven yawns, tiny and perfect, and settles against my chest.

This is real. This is mine.

Not because I was lucky. Because I was brave enough to kneel. To trust. To say yes when every instinct told me to run.

Yeah, I can live with this forever.

The End

ABOUT APRIL CROSS

I'm a writer of spicy stories... okay, I'll be honest, most of my stuff is ghost pepper spicy. I started writing wife sharing stories under Lacey Cross before branching out to longer romantic erotica. I write power play stories with guys who demand to be in control.